KEEPING SECRETS

Other Books by Jill Ammon Vanderwood

Through the Rug: Tenth Anniversary Edition

Through the Rug 2: Follow that Dog Tenth Anniversary Edition

Through the Rug 3: Charm Forest

What's it Like, Living Green? Kids Teaching Kids, by the Way They Live

Drugs Make You Un-Smarter

Shaking Behind the Microphone: Overcoming the Fear of Public Speaking

Erase the Problem of Bullying

Santa's Mysterious Boot: Finding the True Spirit of Christmas

The Year Santa Lost His List

The San Francisco Adventures of Sara the Pineapple Cat

Off Target: The Path You Choose #1

On the Rocks: The Path You Choose #2

Cheers: The Path You Choose #3

KEEPING SECRETS

The Path You Choose - #4

Jill Ammon Vanderwood

Illustrated by Kerah Diez

Idea Creations Press

www.ideacreationspress.com

Published by Idea Creations Press LLC.

LIBRARY OF CONGRESS CATALOGING-IN-PUBLICATION DATA
Names: Vanderwood, Jill Ammon, author
Title: Keeping Secrets: The Path You Choose #4 / Jill Ammon Vanderwood
Description: First edition. | Salt Lake City: Idea Creations Press, 2023.
Identifiers: LCCN 2023912053 ISBN 978-1948804318
Subject: The Path You Choose | Secrets |Choices | Social Issues |Young Adult Fiction: School & Education

www.ideacreationspress.com

Dedication

I dedicate this book to brave girls who tell their secrets and make a difference in their lives and for those around them. To those willing to help and build awareness of the problems plaguing young women today.

Acknowledgments

I am grateful for my editor, Michele G. at Upwork. Her insights have greatly improved my work. I want to thank my very talented illustrator, Kerah Diez. I give her my text, and she makes thoughtful suggestions. Her finished work speaks for itself! A thank you to my remarkable and talented publisher, Douglas Jones from Idea Creations Press! Thank you to my support groups at the League of Utah Writers and The Society of Children's Book Writers and Illustrators. And thanks to my husband, Bill Vanderwood. We've always made a great team!

Keeping Secrets: The Path You Choose #4

Story Guide

Beginning: Page O picture, 1, and choice page 2

Story 1—Layla's Secret—Layla Tells Her Mom: pages 1,2,3, 6 picture, 7 10, 11, 18, 19, 22

Story 2 Layla Tells Her Dad—pages 1,2, 3,5, 14 picture, 15, 28, 29

Story 3 Everly's Secret—Everly tells her pastor—pages 1,2, 4, 8, 24 picture, 25, 31, 32, 39, 40, 46, 47, 52, 56, 57

Story 4 Everly Doesn't Tell Anyone—pages 1, 2, 4, 8, 24, 25, 31, 32, 9, 20, 21, 34 picture, 35, 41, 42, 50, 51, 60, 61

Story 5 Skylee's Secret—Should she confront her parents? Pages 1, 2, 38, 44 picture, 45, 58, 59, 67, 68, 69, 77, 78, 79, 82, 83

Story 6 Should Sklyee Continue to Live with Her Parents? Pages 1, 2, 38, 44 picture, 45, 58, 59, 36, 37, 48 picture, 49, 54 picture, 55, 62, 76 ending.

Story 7 Mia's Secret—pages 1, 2, 64 picture, 65, 70, 71, 86, 87, 88, 92, 93, 98, 99, 100

Story 8 Mia Won't Tell on Her Brother—pages 1,2, 64 picture, 65, 70, 71, 86, 26, 27, 43, 53, 74 picture, 75, 80, 81, 90, 91

Story 9 Harper's Secret—pages 1, 2, 12, 13, 30, 33, 84 picture, 85, 96, 97, 108, 109, 111, 112, 113

Story 10 Your Mom's Secret—pages 1, 2, 89, 94 picture, 95, 102, 103, 106

Story 11 Ava's Secret—pages 1, 2, 101, 116 picture, 117, 121, 122, 123, 126, 127, 147

Story 12 What is Kaylee Hiding? Pages 1, 2, 4, 16, 17, 66, 114 picture, 115, 107, 120

Story 13 Harper's Guess—pages read story 12 on pages 1, 2, 4, 16,17, 66, 114 picture, 115, 107, 120 (which is story 12), and then continue with Harper's Guess on page 23, 63, 72 picture, 73

Story 14—part 1, You Follow Kaylee—pages 1.,4,16, 17, 66, 114 picture, 115, 107, 120 (which is story 12), and then story 14 begins on page 105, 118 picture, 119, 128,129, 137

Story 14—part 2, You Think You Know Kaylee's Secret—read story 14 part one on pages 105, 118 picture, 119, and 128, and then switch to story 14, part two on page 130,132, and 136

Story 15 What is Kaylee's Secret?—Pages 1, 2, 4, 8,131, 133, 138 picture, 139, 140, 141, 142, 143, 146—this can be read at anything after you begin story 3—but it is recommended that you first read stories 12—What is Kaylee hiding? and 13, Harper's Guess, as well as stories 14 part 1--You Follow Kaylee and 14 part 2—You think you know Kaylee's Secret. But. . . there are some who can't wait to read the ending, so there's that possibility too.

Story 16 Does Kaylee Tell You Her Secret? Pages 1, 2, 4, 8, 131, 138 picture, 139, 140, 141, 142, 143, 146, (which is story 15), and then continue with pages 124 picture, 125, 134 picture, 135, 110, 104, 144 picture 145. This chapter sums up all the stories and guesses about Kaylee, so it is best to be read last.

You are a middle school aged girl. You have a group of friends who always eat lunch together at school. It's your birthday and you are planning a slumber party. Each of your seven friends has let you know they can come. Your mom is working in the kitchen, preparing snacks for you and your friends. The doorbell rings and you run to answer it.

It's your friend Kaylee. She has her sleeping bag and overnight bag. You show her into the family room, where you and your friends will sleep. Your friends Skylee, Everly, Harper, Layla and Ava are arriving. You are still waiting for Mia, who arrives soon after.

One of your favorite things to do is to talk about the boys you have a crush on. When you get to that topic, Kaylee is quiet. You wonder what's bothering her.

As the night goes on with dressing up and singing for TikTok videos, you decide to try a new game. "Okay everyone, it's time to tell your deepest, darkest secret. But first, everyone in this room needs to promise that it will stay in this room, and no one will talk about it to anyone else!"

You ask, "Kaylee, do you promise?"

She turns bright red. Hangs her head slightly and says "Yes."

"Skylee?"

"Yes, of course!"

This story continues on page 2.

"Everly?"

"Absolutely!"

"Harper?"

"Yes, I promise."

"How about you Mia?"

"Yes, I do. I promise to keep the secrets."

"What about you, Lala?"

She motions as if to cross her heart, and says, "I cross my heart!"

"Ava?"

"Wait, we are telling our secrets?"

"Yes. Do you promise not to tell other people's secrets?"

"Yes, I promise not to tell, but I'm not sure I want to tell mine."

"Okay Ava, that's up to you. And I promise that what is said in this room, stays here," you say.

What happens next is up to you. It's time to choose your path.

Continue with story 1 on **page 3**—for Layla's Secret.

Turn to **page 4** to begin Everly's Secret, in story # 3.

Turn to **page 38** to begin Skylee's Secret in story # 5

Turn to **page 64 and 65** to begin Mia's Secret, in story #7

Turn to **page 12** to begin Harper's Secret, in story # 9

Turn to **page 89** to begin Your Mom's Secret, in story #10

Turn to **page 117** to begin Ava's Secret # 11.

"Let's form a circle and start with Lala."

Layla looks at you and says, "Okay, but why does it always have to start with me?"

"At least you will get it over with."

A tear runs down Layla's cheek, she begins to shake and then she speaks.

"One day when I was at school, I realized that I forgot my gym clothes, so I got permission from the office to go home and get them. I knew my parents would be working so I didn't bother to call anyone. When I got to the house, my mom's car was in the driveway, along with another car."

There isn't another sound in the room as everyone listens for what Layla will say next. "I opened the front door with my key and walked inside. I didn't see anyone in the living room or the kitchen, except there were two unfinished glasses of wine on the kitchen table. Next, I saw different pieces of clothing lying on the floor. There was a shoe here and a sock there. Some things looked like they belonged to my mom, such as her blouse and high heel shoes. Other things looked like they belonged to a guy, but not my dad."

This story continues on pages 6 and 7

When it's Kaylee's turn to tell her secret. You notice that she is slowly backing away from the group. She isn't saying anything.

"Kaylee, it's your turn to tell your secret."

"I'm not," she says, getting to her feet. "I'm sorry about what happened to Layla! I really am. I can't. I just can't share my secret, ever! I've got to go now," she bursts into tears and runs from the room. You all turn toward the door and then you hear the front door slam as well. Kaylee is gone.

"Whoa! Something bad must have happened to Kaylee!" you say. "Okay, I will go next. I don't have anything bad to say.

In fact, I'm glad my secret is harmless. All I can think of is that I keep forgetting to bring home my science book to study and now I'm facing a D on my midterm. My parents expect me to get As or Bs, but I've been lazy. I need to get all kinds of extra credit to bring my grade up before my parents find out."

Everly, who has been quiet and keeps nodding off suddenly sputters, "Oh really! You think that's bad? You think that's a secret? Really!"

Mia gives Everly a sideways look, "Well, that's something."

What happens next is up to you! It's time to choose a path.
Will you continue to find out Everly's Secret? Continue story 3 on **page 8.**

Do you wonder What is Kaylee Hiding? Begin story #12 on **page 16**

Layla's mother doesn't know that Layla saw something going on in the house when she came home to get her gym clothes. Layla decides to tell her dad what she saw.

"Dad, on Monday I forgot my gym clothes at home. I didn't call anyone to bring them to me because I thought you and Mom would be at work. I got permission to leave school and when I got home, I saw Mom's car in the driveway. I was surprised she was home, but I also saw another car parked behind hers."

"Oh, really, I wonder who was at the house. I will have to ask your mom about that."

"Well Dad, I don't know whose car that was. The thing is, when I came into the house, there were two wine glasses on the table. What I saw next was even worse."

"What is it, Layla?"

"There were pieces of clothing draped around the room and up the stairs as well. Not just Mom's clothes, but also, a man's clothing."

Her dad gasps! "Did you see anything? Hear anything?"

"Yes, I heard Mom giggling, and I heard a man's voice saying, 'You are so beautiful!'"

This story continues on pages 14 and 15.

"I didn't see anyone, and I didn't want anyone to see me, so I quietly walked up the steps to my parent's room. The door was closed but I heard voices coming from the room. My mom was giggling, and a man's voice told her she was beautiful!"

"No!" said Harper. "What did you do?"

"That's my mom!" says Layla. "I immediately went into my room, grabbed my gym clothes, and then got out of there, quickly. I don't know why I feel like I'm the guilty one, but I do. I don't know what to do."

"Layla, you should talk to your mom," says Everly.

"No, no," says Skylee. "I think you should tell your dad."

"I don't know," says Lala. "I wonder if I should keep my mom's secret. If I tell her that I know, she will either ask me to keep it quiet or make me promises that I'm not sure she will keep. But if I tell my dad, it might break up their marriage."

"But Layla, do you want your dad to stay with a cheater?" you ask.

"No, but I love my mom," Layla wails. "You all promised not to tell, but maybe you can help me decide what to do."

What should Layla do? It's time to choose a path.
Does Layla confront her mom? Continue with story 1 on **page 10.**
Does Layla tell her dad? Begin story 2 on **page 5.**

Mia says to you, "At least you know it's a problem and now you have time to fix it if you work hard. Besides, no one has the right to say that someone else's secret is dumb, okay?"

What happens next is up to you! It's time to choose a path
Everly's Secret continues with story 3 on **pages 24 and 25**.
Begin Mia's Secret with story 7 on **page 64**.
Do you want to skip ahead and read, What is Kaylee's Secret? Begin story 15 on **page 131**.

You tried to be supportive of Everly. You offered to go with her to talk to someone about getting help, but she refused. You and those in your group from the slumber party are the only ones who know about Everly's secret. Without getting help, you are beginning to see her crash.

When she comes to school, she looks like she hasn't slept for days. Her hair is dirty, her clothes look like she hasn't washed them, and she won't make eye contact with anyone. She used to be on the cheer squad and go to all the games. She had a boyfriend on the football team.

Everly doesn't even hang out with you anymore.

Rather than getting help to stop the addiction, Everly is moving on toward criminal activity. When you last talked to her, she knew she was addicted, and she was running out of pills. You know she stays out most of the night and drinks with her brother and his drug dealer friend. She is avoiding you, because you know her secret, and you want her to get help.

Apparently, she's not ready for help. If Everly hasn't stolen a car yet, you know it's about to happen and you must do something to stop it. If she won't help herself, you have to step in. You call a meeting after school to see if any of your friends, who also know the secret, have heard anything new from or about Everly.

This story continues on page 20.

After the slumber party, when Layla is alone in the kitchen with her mother, she says, "Mom, the other day I came home to get my gym clothes. I didn't call you because I thought you would be at work."

"What day was that?" asks her mother.

"It was Monday, remember? The day that you weren't at work, and you weren't alone in the house either."

"Oh! That day. So did you see or hear anything, honey?"

"Yes, Mom, I did! I saw two wine glasses on the table. I also saw pieces of clothing down the hall and up the steps. Do you want me to continue?"

Layla's mom turns red. "No, honey that won't be necessary. I could try to say that things aren't what they seem, but that won't help."

"Mom, how could you break up our family like this?"

"Layla, I know this is upsetting but you will have to trust me when I say I love you and your brother, and I don't want to break up the family. But it really might be the best thing for all of us."

"No Mom. No! I can keep a secret if you promise that you will end it."

"No, Layla. I can't promise that. I won't promise that, but I can promise it won't happen in this house again. Will that help?"

This story continues on page 11.

Quietly, Layla says, "This will hurt Dad and it's hurting me. I can't be a part of your lie. You are my mom and I love you, but this? It's too much. If you didn't love Dad, then why didn't you leave before something like this happened?"

"I would have. I should have, but I kept thinking I would end it. I just never did. I didn't want to hurt anyone. I really didn't. What will you do now? Will you tell your dad?"

"No Mom, you need to tell Dad. It's not my secret to tell. It's yours, you tell Dad."

"I will tell him, I promise, but I won't do it now. I need to think about the best way to say it, so it won't hurt as badly."

"There isn't a best way to tell him Mom. There isn't a best time to tell him and there's no way to stop it from hurting Dad, me, or my brother. You had plenty of time to think about this. So, let's get it over with."

The next day, Layla is pretty sure her parents have not talked. Dad has just left for work without slamming the door. In fact, he kissed her mom before leaving.

Layla's mom didn't get dressed for work this morning. Rather than getting ready for work, her mother goes upstairs to pack a suitcase. Layla is thinking, *she isn't going to talk to Dad. She's just going to leave!*

This story continues on page 18

Your friends have taken turns telling secrets, which you have all sworn not to share. Now it's time for Harper to tell her secret.

"This is a very hard secret, but I think it's best to just say it quickly before I chicken out. Um, I was molested by my uncle Paul when I slept over at my cousin's house. I never told my parents since I didn't want to end the friendship I had with my favorite cousin."

"Harper, when did this happen?" asks Mia.

"It happened when I was ten, the first time. But then it happened again last year when we had a family Christmas party, at my house."

"Did you tell anyone? Did you at least tell your cousin?" you ask.

"No, no I didn't tell anyone. I just kept it a secret. He told me that he was everyone's favorite uncle, and no one would even believe me."

"Oh my gosh, Harper!" says Layla. "That's terrible! I think you should tell someone. For one thing, your cousin lives in the house with the pervert, and she may have been molested by her own dad, ever since she was little. Did you think of that? Do you have any other girl cousins?"

"Yes, there's little Deja who is five and Nia is seven."

This story continues on page 13.

This story continues on page 13.

"Please, please tell someone Harper. Either tell your cousin, your mom, or your dad. Or, if you want, you can talk to my mom," you say. "She usually knows what to do."

"I think I could talk to your mom, since she's not involved with my family."

"Okay, good. Will you promise to take my mom's advice, even if it's uncomfortable?"

"Yes, okay. I will take her advice, I promise."

You call your mother into the family room where you are having the slumber party.

"Mom, Harper has a problem, and she needs to ask you for advice. Can you talk to her?" All of your friends remain in the room and listen quietly.

"Sure, honey. What's bothering you Harper? I've known you since kindergarten. You can talk to me."

"Well, I feel so stupid talking to you about this. I know it's not my fault, but if it's not, then why do I feel so guilty?"

"What is it, Harper?"

"I have a favorite cousin named Jada. We grew up together and we would spend the night with each other.

When I was ten, my uncle Paul molested me when I was at their house. He touched me in sexual ways and tried to kiss me like he would with his wife."

"Oh, my! Did you tell your parents?"

This story continues on page 30.

Layla's Dad is visibly shaken. Tears run from his eyes. "Layla, honey have you told your mom what your saw and heard?"

"No, Dad!"

"Okay, you say that was on Monday, right?"

"Yes, it was Monday."

"Next Monday, I will go to the house about that same time and see if I can catch anything going on. Don't say anything to your mom about this, okay?"

"Okay, Dad. I will keep the secret and let you handle it."

Layla lets her friends know that she told her dad, and for now the secret is safe. No one will tell her mom that they know what's going on at the house, while the family isn't there.

On Monday at about 10:00 AM, when Layla is at school and her mom should be at work, Layla's dad stops his car a few houses down and waits and watches. At 10:20, first his wife's car pulls into the driveway, followed by a black sedan. He takes out his binoculars and focuses on the house. The man who gets out of the car is his wife's co-worker, Stan Goodman. He knows him well.

Her dad watches and gives them some time before creeping up toward his own kitchen windows. He watches the two chatting and drinking wine at the kitchen table. He then backs off and sits in the backyard to wait for about fifteen minutes.

This story continues on page 28.

The group of friends from the slumber party know that Kaylee has a secret. When it came time for her to tell her secret to the group, Kaylee ran out of the room saying, "I will never tell my secret. Never!" You all heard the door slam as she left the house.

You offer, "I know she's going out at night because Kaylee told her mother that she was spending the night at Mia's house one night and my house another time. But when her mom called my house, she wasn't staying here. So, where is she going at night?"

Mia says, "I want to guess. I say her dad is in the Mafia and he's training her in how to dispose of a body. Let's look through the paper to see if there are any missing persons."

Ava tells her, "Mia, I don't think she's sneaking out with her dad, because that wouldn't be sneaking out. If she was with her dad, then she wouldn't make up a story about staying over at your house, when she really wasn't."

"Well, yeah. That's true. But I still want to find out about missing persons reports."

Layla says, "Have you noticed that Kaylee is gaining weight?"

"Wait, oh yeah, maybe a little bit."

Layla continues, "My guess is that Kaylee is taking secret Karate lessons and she gained weight because she started taking steroids."

This story continues on page 17.

Everyone agrees. "Yes, that could be it. But why would someone be sneaking around so they could take Karate lessons?" you say.

"But, if she was taking steroids, she definitely wouldn't want us to know, right?" Ava says.

"Do girls take steroids?" asks Harper.

"Yes, I think they do. Don't you remember when some of the Olympic athletes were kicked out of the completion for doping?" says Skylee.

"Oh, yeah. I think girls take it to make themselves stronger or faster," adds Mia.

You say, "Okay, so let's say that Kaylee is learning Karate, and taking steroids."

"Yeah," says Ava. "I say that Kaylee is being bullied at school. She wants to get strong so the bullies will leave her alone. She does that by taking steroids and taking Karate lessons. "What should we do?"

Layla suggests, "We find out about the symptoms of steroid use in girls. Then we follow her to see where she goes at night. And we should confront her about it. Then we offer to help her with the bully and her addiction to steroids."

Everly looks up the effect that steroids have on your appetite.

This story continues on page 66.

Layla leaves for school, and she knows in her heart that her mom won't be there when she gets home. Where will her mother go? Will she go to the mysterious guy's house to live? Will she go on a trip to some foreign place, or will she move into her own apartment?

Layla thinks, *why did I have to talk to my mother? Why didn't I just leave things alone? It's all my fault. I caused the breakup of my parents! Now I can't fix things. I can never make things right.*

When your group of friends see Layla at school, she tells all of you that things aren't going well.

Mia convinces her to call her dad and tell him what is going on. "Maybe he can catch your mom before she leaves without a word."

Layla calls her dad at his work. You and Mia stand with her for support.

"Dad, I really need to talk to you. Mom didn't go to work today, and I saw her packing a suitcase. I think she's going to leave us."

Her dad says, "What, honey? She seemed fine this morning. What makes you think your mother would leave us?"

This story continues on page 19.

"Dad, I think she has a boyfriend. She was with someone when I came home from school to get my gym clothes. There were two wine glasses and men's clothing. I asked mom about it and told her to talk to you, and she said she would, but I think she's just going to leave instead. If you go home now, at least you can talk to her."

Layla's dad is quiet for a moment. "Layla, I believe you. Thank you for telling me, but this is shocking news for me. My heart is broken because I love your mother dearly. That must have been a heavy secret for you to carry around. After what you saw, I know she's involved with someone else. I don't think I can stop her from leaving, but at least she will have to talk to me. I'll go home now and see what she has to say."

Before they hang up her father says, "Layla, I need you to know this is not your fault! You didn't cause it and there's no way you can stop it. Let me take care of things now. No matter what, you and your brother will always be my priority. I love you sweetheart!"

"I love you too, Daddy!"

Layla's dad goes home to talk to her mom. After school her dad tells her and her brother, "Your mom and I are going to separate, at least for a while. Mom will move into an apartment. It's better for us to live apart until things can be figured out. For now, you will both live in this house with me. You can still see your mom and stay with her every other weekend."

This story continues on page 22.

When your friends show up to your house for the meeting, you begin by saying, "We need to do something to help Everly. If we don't, she might spend the next few years in detention, or running from the law."

You continue, "Everly isn't getting any better. I offered to go with her to talk with her pastor or to the school counselor, but she wouldn't go."

"But, you know, we all promised her we wouldn't tell anyone," says Harper. "We won't be true friends if we get her into trouble."

"No. You are wrong. We won't be true friends if we sit by and allow her to ruin her life. You all heard the story. Everly is taking drugs and drinking. Those habits were created by her own brother and his drug dealer friend. Now that she's hooked, they want her to pay. Her payment is high. Everly is being forced to steal a car. She can't make a change in her addiction without help. If she didn't want help, she wouldn't have told us about it."

"I agree," says Mia. "She wants help. We are the only ones who know, so we are the only ones who can help her, before it's too late. I may have to get my own brother in trouble, and she probably will have to tell someone what *her* brother is doing. I still hope we can help Everly."

This story continues on page 21.

You started out with seven friends and now you are down to four. Skylee is busy solving her own problems. Everly won't speak to anyone, so you are trying to help her, and Kaylee is the one who left the group during the slumber party, when you were just beginning to tell secrets. You still wonder what secret she is keeping.

You say, "We can get the help that Everly won't. It doesn't matter if she hates us for doing it. We will either go to her mom, her pastor, or her school counselor. Who is with me?"

"I am," says Mia.

"Me too!" says Harper.

"Okay, who should we talk to?" asks Ava?

"So, how can we help her?" you ask.

Layla says, "Let's start out with the school counselor and if that doesn't help, let's go to her pastor. Either the counselor or the pastor can be the one to tell her mother, so we won't have to."

The next day before school the five of you meet at the front door of the school. Then you go together to talk to Everly's school counselor.

This story continues on pages 34 and 35.

It wasn't the secret that ruined the happy family Layla thought she knew. The problem wasn't solved by telling her mom what she saw, but at least no one is going on living a lie and pretending that everything is great, while Layla must live with a painful secret.

Once the secret got out, the family could start dealing with it and moving on.

Layla is so glad she has good friends to talk to about her secret.

The End 1, 2

Story 1 has ended, but there are still more secrets to tell.

It's time to choose a new path. What secret will you choose next?

If you wish to learn more of Layla's story, begin story 2—Layla Tells Her Dad on **page 5**.

If you wish to learn Skylee's Secret, begin story 5 on **page 38**.

Harper says, "I know what Kaylee is doing. She's hiding a runaway girl in her bedroom."

"But Harper, that doesn't explain why she is going out at night or the fact that she is gaining weight, does it?

"Well, she is going around with a different friend. Her name is Paisley. And it looks like they are catching the bus to school together. Paisley often wears Kaylee's clothes, so she could be living in Kaylee's closet or under her bed at night. I also see Kaylee going to the store and coming back with two of everything. Two drinks, two hotdogs, and two bags of chips. So, I say she is hiding Paisley and that Paisley is a runaway!"

Skylee says, "I say she's going out at night and tagging. The reason I say that is because she is hanging out with Paisley a lot, and Kaylee is always drawing, that means she loves art. So, art, plus a new friend—who may also love art plus Kaylee sneaking out of the house at night when she says she's with you or Mia. That all adds up to secretly tagging."

"Okay, then let's put that all together," you say. "Kaylee has a secret new friend, in fact, they wear each other's clothes a lot. That girl is a runaway who secretly lives in Kaylee's room. Kaylee makes trips to the store and comes back with extra drinks, chips, and hotdogs, so that's why she is gaining weight."

This story continues on page 63.

Everly turns to you, "You think you have a problem because you almost got a D in science. You poor girl! You think you have it bad?"

You get embarrassed and start to turn red.

Everly continues, "My neighborhood is alive at night. When our parents think I'm in bed, I'm out with my brother and a couple of guys next door, drinking!"

All of your friends' gasp.

"That's right. This one guy they call Fix, and my brother Sam steal cars for a living. They have so much money that they provide the rest of us with alcohol and drugs. I started out drinking when I was twelve and now it's pills. I'm not sure, but I think I might be addicted."

You ask, "But what about school? I see you at school most of the time."

"Yes, but am I *really* at school?"

"What do you mean?"

"Think about the D you are getting in science and multiply that by seven classes. I might be there but after staying up most of the night, I need to sleep sometime, right?"

"Everly, what are you saying?" asks Mia.

This story continues on page 31.

Mia is too afraid to do anything. She is in a hard spot, with her brother involved in a hit and run accident. She also knows that the car Ray was driving belongs to her parents. Her parents keep asking about the car. She hasn't told them anything, but she will soon be forced to make some hard choices.

You and your friends swore to keep Mia's secret, but you wonder if you should go against your friend Mia and turn her brother in. Or should you report the car? What her brother did *is* a crime. The vehicle is in a safe place for now, but someone is bound to spot the wrecked car.

When the police find the missing car, will they find the victim's blood?

No matter what you and your friends say to Mia, she refuses to report the crime.

You call your other friends to your house for a meeting, to talk this through.

After they arrive you begin the conversation. "What should we do about Mia? She is a witness to a crime that her brother Ray committed. Mia knows that a woman is lying unconscious in a hospital bed. The woman might die! We know something that could help the police solve a crime. What should we do?"

Layla speaks up, "There are professional people who can help us, and they are protected by client or patient confidentiality, or secrecy. One professional is a doctor."

Harper says, "That's right! A lawyer is also sworn to secrecy and so is a minister."

This story continues on page 27.

"Or we could tell our parents and have them help us with this," you say.

Skylee says, "Mia might know that we told someone, and we said we wouldn't. Mia should be the one to tell someone, not us."

The next day, the four of you ride your bikes over to where the car is hidden. You look at the front bumper and you are sure you can see traces of blood. There is also a scrap of cloth on the bumper, which could be part of the injured woman's clothes.

You and Ava go to Mia's house and try one more time to talk her into telling someone about the secret.

At first, she doesn't budge. You tell her "I know that we promised not to tell your secret, but even though I know it's not my problem, I feel like I need to tell someone."

Mia stands up and begins to shout at you. "You promised! You promised! Get out. I don't need friends like you!"

You and Ava get up to leave Mia's house, but before you go, Ava says. "A minister is sworn to secrecy. It's called a confidentiality clause. But if the police know someone confessed to a murder, the court couldn't force the minister to tell on that person."

This story continues on page 43.

Then Layla's dad goes around to the front door and opens it with his key. He quietly steps inside and looks around the room. There is no sign of anyone in the kitchen or the living room. He does see the telltale signs of clothing on the floor from the kitchen to the top of the stairs. He knows he has caught them. He lights a match to set off the fire alarm and waits for them to come out of the bedroom at the top of the stairs.

All at once the house is on alert with the wailing of the fire alarm. First his scantily dressed wife comes from the room, followed by her 'friend,' who is nearly undressed as well.

Layla's dad is standing near the front door, with his arms crossed. A look of terror washes over their faces when they see Layla's dad standing by the door. They have been caught!

Layla's dad knows she wouldn't leave him, and he also knows that he doesn't want to deal with an unfaithful wife.

"You have a few choices," he says, "You can end this right now and we can go on living our life and raising our children, or you can move in with this married man and his wife. Or whatever plan you can come up with."

This story continues on page 29.

Layla's dad continues, "I am leaving now. I've seen enough. I will be in touch with Stan's wife Marjorie, to let her know what I just witnessed at my house. You may not think you are hurting anyone with this little playdate, but you are wrong."

He continues, "... Layla came home last Monday and saw two cars in the driveway. She also saw two wine glasses, and clothes strewn around the room and up the stairs. She heard giggles and voices coming from the bedroom. I told her I would handle this. And now, it appears that I have.

What a heavy burden you have put on your daughter. She thinks she's the one who is breaking up our family."

Later, Layla's dad tells his daughter, "The only way things will go back to normal is if the family goes through counseling, and your mom agrees to stop cheating."

Layla is torn between her parents in the divorce, but she chooses to stay in her own home with her dad and her brother. That way she can go to the same school and keep her friends, especially you. You are glad you encouraged Layla to tell her dad.

The End 3

You have just finished reading Layla's Secret, which was included in stories 1 and 2.

It's time to choose a new path and learn a different secret!

If you wish to continue with story # 3, Everly's Secret turn to **page 4**.

If you wish to hear Your Mom's Secret, begin story 10 on **page 89**.

For Harper's Secret, begin story 9 on **page 12**.

"No, I didn't tell anyone, but I made sure I didn't stay at their house again. I only had sleepovers with Jada at my own house after that."

Your mom says, "I'm so sorry that happened to you Harper. I'm also sorry you didn't feel like you could tell anyone. Has it ever happened to you again?"

"Yes," says Harper. "Last Christmas when we had a family party at my house. I had to go to the bathroom, and my uncle caught me alone and tried the same thing with me again."

"I'm worried that he might try something with my younger cousins. I am also worried that he may be molesting my cousin Jada, who is his daughter. I haven't dared to ask anyone about this. Now I think I should do something. What should I do?"

"You're right, Harper. If you were molested, then your other cousins are likely to have the same problem."

"How do you feel about telling your parents?"

"If my dad found out, I think he would kill Uncle Paul."

Your mom stands in front of Harper. She looks straight into her eyes and tells her, "Without talking, this won't go away. Do you understand that?"

This story continues on page 33.

"I'm saying that you once knew me as a good girl. I mean, I had once been a choir girl at my church, but now I'm pretty sure that Fix and my brother have not done me any favors. I think I'm an addict at this point. The future that could have been bright for me may just be washed up!"

Everly continues, "I don't even know how to come back from this mess!" Everly takes a container of water from her backpack and opens a bottle of pills. She first takes out one pill then shrugs and adds one more to her hand before swallowing.

No one knows what to say for a minute.

"Everly, does you mom know?" asks Skylee.

"No, she doesn't, but when she gets my report card, she will know something is wrong. And it won't just be a D."

"What about your brother. What does he do?" asks Layla.

"He parties all night. At least I go home by about 2:00 AM. Then when I go to school, I'm pretty sure he sleeps all day and then starts over the next night."

"Everly, do you want to continue this way?" asks Ava.

This story continues on page 32.

"No, No I don't. I just don't know what to do. I don't know how to get help and I don't know how to stop. What do you think I should do? Now that I'm hooked on pills, my brother and Fix, want me to start stealing cars, 'to pay for the drugs.' How can I steal cars when I'm not even old enough to drive? I just don't know how this will ever get better."

You offer, "Everly, I can help or support you, but first you need to tell someone. You can either talk to your pastor, a teacher, counselor, or your parents."

"So, even if I talk to my pastor, I will still have to tell my parents, right?"

Harper speaks up, "Well, yeah, but it may help to tell your pastor first. He can give you advice and even go with you to tell your parents, so you won't be alone. Since you are under eighteen, you can't just check yourself into rehab. I think you will need your parent's help and their permission."

What should Everly do? It's time to choose a path.
Everly tells her pastor about her problems. Continue story 3 on **page 39**.
Everly Doesn't Tell Anyone. Begin story 4 on **page 9**.

"Uh, yes."

"How about if I arrange a meeting with you, and your parents?"

Harper says, "Um, I guess. If you and my friends will be there. I think I can handle it."

"After that, you will need to file a police report. Would you be willing to do that?"

"Oh, I don't know. I don't think my uncle is a criminal," says Harper.

"Yes, Harper. Your uncle is a criminal. An adult who molests a child is a criminal. Do you think it's okay for him to continue doing this to other little girls?"

"Well, no."

"Harper, you are so brave! Some women continue to live with a secret like this until they are grown-up, and the molester is an old man. It continues to haunt them for their whole life when it could have been handled and stopped many years earlier."

"Yes, I will talk to my parents. I promised your daughter and my other friends that I would take whatever advice you gave me. I will."

Your mom goes into the kitchen and makes a call to Harper's mom. She asks for them to come to your house the next evening.

This story continues on pages 84 and 85.

You speak up first. "We have a friend who isn't doing very well. Her name is Everly Emmet, and we think she might be on drugs."

"Everly Emmet? And you think she might be on drugs?"

Without coming right out with the secret, Mia speaks up. "We were having a slumber party and we saw her taking some pills. At school we noticed that she is always sleeping in class."

"Okay, what if the pills are just Tylenol? That would make it very awkward for me to accuse her of taking pills, wouldn't it?"

You tried the easier way. But now it's important to get the message out.

Harper blurts out, "she told us a secret that she has been sneaking out of her house at night and drinking. Her brother's friend is a drug dealer, and he has been giving her pills."

"Now she's addicted, and they want her to start paying for the drugs by stealing cars," you finish.

"We told her to tell someone and get help, but we've seen her the past few days, when she does come to school, and she isn't doing well," says Ava.

This story continues on page 41.

Skylee told her secret, that the people she is living with, the mom and dad she has always known, might not be her parents after all.

Skylee thinks about the times her parents have been there for her. When she skinned her knees, her mom cleaned her up and sang to her until she felt better. When Skylee lost her first tooth, and even when she started her period, her mother was the one who helped her get through it.

Skylee thinks about her dad. He was the one who put training wheels on her bike so she could ride it on her own. He took her to the father-daughter dance at school. She smiles remembering how he helped her count out the money that she saved to buy her puppy from the pet shop.

She knows what the newspaper article means. It means that her loving, caring parents—the only parents she knows, really aren't her parents at all!

How could these people have ever been cruel enough to take a crying child away from her home, her sister and her own Mommy and Daddy? How could they take her from the parents who taught *Jamie* to speak in sentences, and were potty training her?

It just doesn't make sense. Sklyee knows she can't ask them. They won't give her a straight answer. If she brings it up, she worries that they will abandon her, so they won't have to go to jail.

This story continues on page 37.

Skylee doesn't remember being taken when she was two, but now if she is taken away from the parents she loves, at the age of thirteen, that will really hurt!

Skylee decides to talk to her mom. "Mother, I know you said that my birth certificate was lost somehow, but I want to know if I was born in St. Louis?"

"Yes, dear, we have talked about that. After your dad and I got our degrees, we moved away, when you were little."

"Okay," says Skylee. "I will go online and apply for a copy of my birth certificate. I just need to enter my parent's names, birthdate, city, and my birth name. I can have it sent here. I know I will need it, before I can start driver's ed next year."

Her mother stops peeling the potatoes. She is turning pale. She sits down, hard on a kitchen chair. For a moment, she seems to have lost her voice.

Very quietly, her mom says, "No, honey. That won't be necessary. I will take care of it. Don't worry."

This story continues on pages 48 and 49.

You're at the slumber party and Skylee knows it's her turn to share her secret. She tests her voice and begins to talk. "Uh, uh, uh. I don't know what to say, I mean I do know what to say, but I'm not sure if I should really say it out loud. Saying it might make it seem real and I'm not sure I'm ready to face it right now."

She pauses then says, "I don't know if my parents are really my parents."

"What do you mean, Skylee?" asks Everly.

"What I mean is that when I ask my mom for my baby pictures or my birth certificate, she always changes the subject. I don't even know if I have a birth certificate. I've never seen one. My parents have always been very protective of me. They hardly let me out of their sight. So, one day, when my mom wasn't home, I went snooping around and I found something unusual. There was a box under a floorboard in my parent's room. In the box I found an old baby blanket. There was also a toy bunny. As I searched further into the box, I saw a cut-out newspaper article about a missing toddler. I made a copy of the article and I carry it around with me."

She takes a paper out of her bag and begins to read:

This story continues on pages 44 and 45.

Everly decides, "I think we should talk to my pastor. I know that a pastor isn't obligated to tell a secret that is told to him in private. I'm not sure about the teacher or counselor, though."

You make plans with Everly to go with her to see her pastor the following day, on Saturday.

You and Everly ride your bikes to the multi-denominational church which is three blocks away. Everly hasn't made an appointment but when you walk through the doors of the church, you are met with a secretary who asks if she can help you.

Everly says, "Mrs. Clarion, I need to see Pastor Marcus."

"Yes, Everly. It's so good to see you. I will let him know that you are here to meet with him."

The secretary walks away, and you can hear her footsteps repeating down the long hallway. The echo of voices follows and soon there are two sets of footsteps coming back, toward you.

The pastor meets up with you and Everly in the hallway. "Oh, Everly Emmet, it's so good to see you. How may I help you?"

"Oh, um, well, I need to talk," she says.

"Shall we have your friend wait out here?"

"Well, no. I want her to go with me. I need her here."

"Okay, let's go to my office and we will have a chat."

This story continues on page 40.

You and Everly follow Pastor Marcus to his office, where you both sit down. Everly begins to cry. You go over to her with a tissue and try to comfort her.

"What is it, Everly? Is your family well?"

"Yes, Pastor. But I have done something wrong, and I really need to get help."

"Okay, child. Dry your tears. I'm here to listen. And we can pray together."

"Pastor, is it true that you won't tell my parents? Will you keep my secret safe?"

"Yes, Everly. The things you tell me are held in confidence.

However, if it is harmful to keep your secret, I may try to convince you to tell someone. However, the final decision is still yours to make."

"Okay, I've been sneaking out of my house at night and drinking in my neighborhood. I still get up for school in the morning, but I've been too tired to do any of my schoolwork. Now I'm really falling behind."

The pastor nods his head, with both hands together in a steeple. "Okay, I understand how that could really create a problem."

Everly nods her head and becomes so emotional that she can't speak. She points to you, and mouths, "Will you tell him?"

This story continues on page 46.

The counselor stands up and puts her hands on her hips.

"This was told to us as a secret, and we promised not to tell. But now we think that telling might be the only way to save her life or to save her from a life of crime," says Mia.

The counselor says, "You girls did the right thing by telling. Some secrets are very dangerous to keep. I won't tell that you told me, at least at first. I think that by calling her into my office along with her mother, she might even admit to what's going on. I will only speak to her about your suspicions as a last resort. Is that okay?"

"Yes," you all agree and get up to leave. That went better than expected. You say your goodbyes to your friends, then hurry off to class.

The next day Everly is not at school. The following day she does show up. The counselor talks to some of her teachers to see if they are concerned about Everly. They have noticed the same things and also suspect that she is using drugs. The counselor speaks to the principal about this situation and the principal approves a meeting with one Everly's teachers and her counselor, along with Everly and her mom.

When Everly and her mom come to the counselor's office, her counselor begins, "Everly, things aren't the way they always have been with you. Your grades are slipping. In fact, you are not turning in any of your work."

This story continues on page 42.

Her teacher speaks up, "I also notice that you're sleeping in class. Is there a problem at home? Are you getting enough sleep, Everly?"

"I, I'm tired. I'm always tired."

Everly's mom says, "After dinner she goes to her room to do homework. I check on her throughout the evening. She's either playing her guitar and singing or watching TV. I'm sure she is sleeping enough. She hardly goes out or has friends over."

"What do you think the problem is, Everly? You have gone from the honor roll to failing most of your classes."

"I'm too tired to do my homework," she says.

"Why are you so tired?" her mom asks.

Quietly she says, "Because of my brother."

"What? What did your brother do, Everly?"

"I started sneaking out of the house to drink with Sam and his friend. It was fun at first but not anymore. Sam's friend started giving me pills and now I think I'm addicted," says Everly.

Everly's mom gasps and stands up, "Addicted to pills? What kind of pills?"

This story continues on page 50.

You say, "Okay, we are leaving now, and we are going to talk to my minister about your secret. He won't tell anyone what is said to him in private. If you won't go with us, we will go without you. My minister will know what to do."

You are already standing in the doorway, about to leave Mia's house. She has stopped yelling now. She invites you and Ava to come back inside. She then calmly sits down.

"Okay, I agree to tell a minister in a hypothetical way and see what advice he will give me."

You all walk over to the church in your neighborhood. The minister invites each of you to take a seat.

"How may I help you girls?"

You speak up, "This is my friend Mia. She wants to talk to you about something that's bothering her."

"Welcome, Mia!"

Mia begins, "Suppose I know someone who may have committed a crime. And suppose I am a witness, and the person will not turn themselves in. Am I required to tell the police about that crime?"

"Well, in a case where knowing about a crime and telling someone would help the police solve the crime and bring justice to a victim, then the right thing for a witness to do is to tell the police what they know."

This story continues on page 53.

Child Goes Missing from a Supermarket

The mother of young Jamie Kinsley was shopping with her child in the grocery store when she remembered that she didn't pick up milk. She left her cart, where her daughter was seated, down the canned goods aisle and quickly ran back to get the forgotten milk. But on her way back to the cart and her daughter, she saw someone she knew and exchanged a few minutes of conversation. She excused herself and ran back to her child. The child, Jamie, was nowhere to be seen.

Even her toy rabbit and her blanket were missing. After a frantic search of the store by the mother, several store employees and concerned shoppers, they did not find the missing youngster.

Amy Kinsley and her husband are pleading to whoever has their little girl, that they will realize Jamie is better off with her own family, sleeping in her own bed and playing with her older sister.

Jamie Kinsley 2.5 years old, is 34 inches tall, and weighs 26 pounds. Jamie has light blond, curly hair, and blue-green eyes. She is not fully potty trained, and she can talk in short sentences.

If you have any information about Jamie Kinsley's whereabouts or know who took her, please contact the county sheriff's office. All information will be confidential. The family and their church are posting a reward for any information which will lead to Jamie's safe return.

This story continues on page 58.

You open your mouth to speak, "Pastor, Everly wants me to continue for her. She told me that drinking hasn't been the only problem she's having. She's also taking pills that were given to her by her brother Sam and his friend. She doesn't know how to get away from taking drugs and alcohol."

Everly is nodding her head now. She lets you know that she's able to continue.

"I also think my brother and his friend are selling pills, and that's why they have so many drugs to give to me and everyone else. Now that I'm addicted, they want me to commit crimes to pay for my drug habit. They want to train me to steal cars. I know that drinking and taking random pills has gotten me into a mess, and I really need help. I don't know how to get better and to get away from my brother and his friend." She starts to cry again and sobs loudly.

You hold her hand telling her how brave she is.

The pastor is quiet for a few moments. "It's hard to get better from something that has such a hold on you. Now you are considering stealing to support a habit. I'm so glad that you decided to surrender and that you know you can't do this alone. You really do need professional help with this problem."

This story continues on page 47.

Everly very slowly nods her head. "I know that. I really do, but then there is my brother and his friend and all the problems that will come if they get into trouble because of me."

"Everly, the part of the problem that needs immediate attention is your addiction. That's what is messing up everything in your present and if not handled, this can very well mess up your future as well. Do you see the road you are on now?"

"Yes, I do. I can't live without those pills, but I can't afford to take them either, so if this continues, I will become a criminal."

"Do you have such loyalty to your brother Sam, that you are willing to steal for him, so that you can get the pills?"

"Well, yes, he is my brother."

"Did your older brother and his friends look out for you and your best interests?"

"Well, no. They made it look so fun to sneak out at night and drink, but then they gave me pills and I can't stop taking the pills."

"The duty of a parent is to protect and take care of their children. To feed them, clothe them and put a roof over their heads. The duty of an older sibling is like that of a parent, to protect and to defend when a parent is not available. In this case, your older brother has brought harm to you. He isn't looking out for you or your safety."

This story continues on page 52.

The next day while her mom is at work, Skylee goes to her parent's room and removes the box containing the blanket, the stuffed rabbit, and the news article about the kidnapping. This time, she looks more thoroughly for evidence.

Skylee takes out the blanket and looks at it. There is a name, Jamie, and the birthdate, November 21st.

Alarm fills her chest. She has a hard time breathing. *I always celebrate my birthday on May 25th. So, does that mean I was really born on November 21st, the year before?*

Skylee puts the box back under the loose floorboard in her parent's room, before coming to your house.

When you answer the door, Skylee asks you, "Will you help me apply for a birth certificate? I decided to use my birth name and apply for the state of Missouri."

"Sure!"

You log onto the computer and go online for the State of Missouri. On the application she writes the name Jamie Kinsley, born November 21st, in the city of St. Louis, Missouri.

She looks at her copy of the news article for the mother's name: Amy Kinsley.

This story continues on pages 54 and 55.

"I don't know, Mom. Sometimes they are pink and sometimes blue. They made me feel good at first, but now I can't live without them."

Her mom asks, "Do you intend to continue taking pills while letting everything else fall apart around you?"

Now Everly stands up and starts toward the door. The counselor stops her.

She turns toward her mom and says, "I wanted help. I needed help, but who wants to tell on themselves? Who wants to be a baby and tell on their own brother? I don't."

"This problem that I thought would just go away, only got worse, and worse. I hate it!" She sits back down, puts her hands over her face and sobs. Very quietly, she says, "Now Sam and his friend called Fix want me to steal cars to help pay for my addiction."

Her mom gasps! "No, no. How could this be happening right in front of me, and I had no idea?"

The counselor tells Everly's mom about a treatment center where Everly can get help.

"But" she warns, "if someone doesn't stop Sam and his friend, this problem won't end. At some point Everly will be back home, facing the same problem all over again, unless the drug dealer is stopped. Sam did not respect your family values and he didn't protect his younger sister the way an older brother should. Instead, he got her hooked on drugs and then told her she would need to pay for them."

This story continues on page 51.

The school counselor continues, "That means that she will either be forced to steal, sell drugs to other kids or turn to prostitution. It will never end well!"

Everly, who has had her hands over her face, looks up and says, "I am almost out of pills, so I am afraid…"

The counselor says, "I am obligated to report abuse of any form to the authorities. Her brother Sam was abusing his sister. I will need to call the police to pick him up for questioning."

Everly and her mom are very upset and anxious about this phone call. Her mom stands up and starts to say something, "You can't ask me to choose between my children."

Then she shakes her head, as if to clear her thoughts. She sits down, and quietly says, "You're right. If my son is involved in this, and without any thought about the danger he was putting his sister through, he does need to be stopped. It's just hard to turn in my own son."

The counselor says, "I know this is a very hard blow. Your daughter and countless others are in danger for as long as this continues. You aren't the one who is turning him in. That's on me. I have an obligation to protect my student's wellbeing. This is affecting the health and welfare of a student."

She holds out a hand toward Everly, who still has her head down.

This story continues on page 60.

Pastor Marcus asks, "Do you see that?"

"Yes, I do," says Everly.

"If you don't tell your parents about what has happened to you, you are not allowing them to help you or to protect you.

In this case, your parents can't protect your health, and they can't protect your future. If this continues, neither your brother, his friend nor your parents will be able to protect you from the law. A minor, such as yourself can be put into juvenile detention until the age of twenty-one."

The pastor continues, "I know you don't want to go down that road and become a criminal just to protect your brother, who did not protect you. By telling your parents about your drug and alcohol problem, you are fixing your future before everything gets worse. Your brother obviously needs help as well."

Pastor Marcus continues, ". . . with your permission, I would like to pray with you."

Everly says, "Yes, I would like that."

You and Everly close your eyes and bow your heads.

He prays that Everly will have the strength and courage to ask for help and to stay strong even if it means turning her brother in so he can also get help. He ends the prayer with Amen.

You and Everly repeat, "Amen."

This story continues on page 56.

Not satisfied with the minister's advice, Mia presses, "…. but suppose the person who committed the crime didn't know for sure if anyone was hurt? What then?"

"If they didn't know if someone was hurt, then they should at least find out if that person is hurt or not."

Mia asks the minister, "What if they won't?"

He responds, "I would say that if you know about it, you would be the one to make it right."

"Okay, thank you sir! I think I have all the information I was looking for."

"Yes, girls. Thank you for your visit. If someone refuses to do the right thing, then it's our responsibility to make up the difference. We will always feel better, sleep better and even eat better when we have prayed about things and decided to do what is right."

The three of you leave the church and Mia asks you and Ava to go with her to the hospital to see the woman who was injured.

You find out what floor she is on, and you all go to the visiting room on that floor.

This story continues on pages 74 and 75.

"Is it okay if I have my birth records sent to your address? I don't really want my parents to know what I'm doing."

You agree.

When Skylee requests her birth certificate, a flagged notice comes upon the screen, saying: *The birth record you have applied for is not available at this time.*

You and Skylee wonder what that means, until the next day when you receive unexpected visitors to your house.

"FBI," they announce at your door. Their guns are drawn.

"We are looking for a missing girl, Jamie Kinsley. Your address was used to request a copy of the missing girl's birth certificate.

Are you Jamie Kinsley?"

"No, I'm not." You put your hands up and slowly back away from the door. "I know where she lives. She thinks she may have been abducted when she was only two years old."

"It would be best if you don't notify her that we are coming. You could just say, 'I'm coming over. Can you hang out?'"

You text Skylee. *"Hey, can you hang out? Are your parents' home?"*

She texts back. *"No, but Mom will be home any minute."*

"Okay, see you in a bit."

The FBI sends you over to Skylee's house to meet up with her, before her

parents are home. You knock on the door, and she answers.

Only one agent comes to the door with you, while the others sit in an unmarked car, waiting for Skylee's parents to arrive.

This story continues on page 62.

"I can call your mom and ask for her to come to my office. That way you won't have to face this alone. You don't even need to mention the criminal aspect of this problem, just yet. The most important thing is to get help for you, right now! I will also recommend you for treatment in a facility run by a local church. The church can even help with funding if your insurance won't cover the total cost of treatment."

Everly asks, "Can I talk to my friend for a minute?"

Pastor Marcus nods his head, stands up and leaves the room. Everly turns to you, "What do you think I should do?"

"I think you should get help for the addiction before things get much worse, with stealing and dropping out of school or ending up with a criminal record."

"Yes," says Everly. "I think so too." She walks to the door to inform the pastor.

"Okay, pastor. I think we need to call my mom." She is shaking and you aren't sure if she's just afraid or if the drug withdrawal is making her shake.

You are so relieved that Everly is asking for help! It's much better for her to talk to her mom with the pastor present. You leave before Everly's mom arrives.

This story continues on page 57.

Later, Everly calls you, "I want you to know that I'm going to continue the school year at a rehab center."

While she is in treatment, both her brother and her parents attend family sessions. Everly lets the counselors know that it's her brother who has started and contributed to her problems. If Everly comes home to the same living situation, the problems will continue for her, and she will eventually succumb to the addiction again.

Everly is in treatment when arrests are made in her neighborhood. Not only are Sam and Fix arrested for selling drugs, but the leaders of the car theft ring are also rounded up. Everly is sad and glad at the same time to hear this news. She will be going home to a much healthier household and neighborhood.

Everly is now drug free and she is once again getting good grades in school. She is also an active member of her church, and she sings in the choir.

The End 4

You have just finished reading story 3 where Everly talks to her pastor about her secret.

It's time to choose a new path.

Would you like to continue reading Everly's story, Everly Doesn't Tell Anyone else about her secret, and she's starting to crash? Begin story 4 on **page 9**.

"Oh my gosh, Skylee. Do you think that's you?" Mia asks.

"I really don't know, but I think so. My mom says I could talk and sing when I was very young, but I can't remember anything that happened to me when I was that young."

"Could you be adopted, Skylee?" asks Harper.

"Well, even adopted children have birth certificates. They also have some sense of family—like cousins, or grandparents. But I don't. I've never met any other family members."

"Do your parents know that you found the box?" you ask.

"I didn't tell my mom I found the things in her room, but after I copied the news article, I put the original clipping back into the box."

"What are you going to do with it?" asks Ava.

Skylee only shrugs.

"What city was the news article from?" asks Everly.

"It was from St. Louis, Missouri, so that means we must have moved away after that happened. If it happened."

"Your parents can't just keep going with this charade. You will need a birth record to get a job or to get your driver's license," you say.

"It sounds like you have a sister," says Layla.

"I know," says Skylee. "I was thinking about finding her."

This story continues on page 59.

Skylee says "I don't know her name, but her last name is Kinsley. We could look her up on Facebook."

Everyone takes out their phones to look. "Here's an Amy Kinsley. Could she be your mom?" asks Harper. "I mean your real mom."

"Hey, let's look at her family photos." says Mia.

Skylee says, "This is so scary. I'm already shaking."

"OMG. There's a picture of the missing toddler. She had blond curly hair," says Layla.

Skylee holds out a piece of her own curly blond hair which is much longer now.

"Hey guys, you promised not to tell anyone. So now I need to figure this all out. Do I want to go and live with strangers in St. Louis? Do I want to have an older sister? She looks like she might be twenty in these pictures. Do I want my mom and dad to go to jail? It might seem exciting, but to me, it's really, really hard!"

What should Skylee do? It's time to choose a path.

Should she talk to her parents about her birth certificate? Continue story 5 on **page 67.**

Should Skylee Continue to Live with Her Parents, who might have kidnapped her? Begin story 6 on **page 36.**

"Mrs. Emmet, please just go about your day, as if nothing has happened. You do not need to warn Sam that this is taking place. In fact, it will be so much easier for all involved if you don't say anything to him about this. The police will take care of it. If you leave my office now, an officer will come and speak to Everly, and I will handle the whole thing."

Everly's mom is shaking and can't hold back as a sob comes out. Tears are racing down her face. She is trying to blow her nose. She turns to the counselor and squeaks out a, "Thank you! I will leave now, and I won't go home until they take my son, Sam, into custody. I will go to the treatment center to set things up for Everly." She tries to wipe the tears so she can find her way out the office door.

"Everly will be in good hands. Once she speaks to the police, she'll be taken to the treatment center."

Everly will finish out the school year in the treatment center, where she will get help for her addictions.

This story continues on page 61.

Her brother, Sam, is picked up by the police. Everly didn't know his friend's name, but she called him Fix. Her brother told the police where they could find Fix, and he was also picked up with an arsenal of guns, cocaine, marijuana, and a huge assortment of pills. Fix also led them to a place where those higher up from him were running the car theft ring.

It was not too late to get help for Everly because she had not yet stepped into a life of crime.

You, Mia, Harper, Layla and Ava are so glad you all had the courage to speak up and save your friend from a life of crime or even a deadly drug overdose.

The End 5, 6, & 7

You have just read about Everly's secret in stories 3 and 4.
It's time to choose another path and learn another secret.
To learn Skylee's Secret, begin story 5 on **page 38**.
To choose Your Mom's Secret? Begin story 10 on **page 89**.

When Skylee answers the door, an agent shows an FBI badge and tells her, "We received a red flag warning about Jamie Kinsley's birth record. Can you confirm that you are Jamie Kinsley?"

"Uh, yes. I think I'm Jamie. My name has always been Skylee, but I found out that I may have been abducted when I was very young. My parents haven't told me anything, but I have found evidence about the abduction."

"Can you show me the evidence?"

Skylee leads the FBI agent to her parent's bedroom. She lifts the floorboard and pulls out the box with the blanket, the rabbit, and the news article. "I found these and decided to apply for my own birth record with this name.

Do you really think I am this girl?"

"With this evidence, yes."

Skylee shows the agent the certificates where her parents have graduated from college in the state of Missouri. "My mom told me that she used her maiden name for her degree and my dad uses his stepfather's last name now, after he got his degree. Our last name is Williamson." The agent writes down the original names of both parents.

"What will happen to my parents?" Skylee asks.

"We will take your parents in for questioning. In the meantime, you will be placed in DCFS custody. You need to leave the house now, but an officer can come back and pick up anything you want to bring with you."

One moment Skylee is excited to meet her birth parents and she is laughing. Then she remembers that the parents she has known and loved all her life will be arrested and she may never see them again!

This story continues on page 76.

You continue, "but either she's eating both servings of food, or feeding her secret, runaway friend. Both girls slip out at night to go tagging around the neighborhood. Does that cover it, girls?"

They all say "yes!" Mia suggests, "I think we should watch Kaylee again, and see if both girls go to Kaylee's house. We can also watch to see if Kaylee really does buy double snacks and bring them home. We won't know if she's really eating both portions though. We also need to watch and see if they both come out of the house together in the morning before school, and if Paisley is really wearing Kaylee's clothes and shoes."

"Okay," you say, "After that, we need to watch whether they are sneaking out at night. Let's look around the park and the buildings in this area for fresh tagging.

Keep good notes about what you find out."

Mia watches Kaylee's house to see if Paisley comes out of her house with her in the mornings before school. She sees Paisley walking down the sidewalk, toward Kaylee's house. Paisley then goes inside and stays for about fifteen minutes. When they come out, they appear to have swapped clothes; Paisley is wearing different pants and boots, rather than the sneakers she was wearing before. Kaylee is wearing Paisley's pants and sneakers now.

That answers a few questions.

This story continues on pages 72 and 73.

During the slumber party at your house, it's Mia's turn to tell her secret. Unlike the others, who were reluctant, Mia is eager to speak up.

"I'm next. Okay." She holds out her hand as a stop sign. "This really happened to me so please wait before you interrupt. My brother Ray was driving me to the corner store and showing off with his driving. He was also messing around with the car radio. He ran a stop sign and hit something in the road, but we weren't sure if it was a person or a pet."

"But. . ." you start to ask.

"No, no questions, until I'm finished," says Mia. "I started yelling, 'Ray, Ray you hit something. You need to stop! Stop the car now, Ray!' But my brother kept going. He actually sped up. 'Ray, I know you can get in more trouble for hit and run.' We were heading for the store, but we didn't go to the store at all. My brother just went down a few blocks to an abandoned building and parked his car behind the building at the edge of a field. He then told me not to breathe a word of it to anyone." Mia motions with her hands, "And here I am, telling this secret to all of you when my brother said that I'm an accomplice and we could both get into big trouble!"

This story continues on page 70.

Everly then reports to the group, "I found out that steroids change your metabolism, increase your appetite, and increase fat. So, steroids can cause a person to have a fat belly, unless they exercise a lot."

Harper says, "I will check to see if Kaylee eats a lot. I'll follow her at school and write down everything Kaylee eats for lunch."

Skylee watches to see if Kaylee exercises a lot. "I will find out if she walks to school. Does she take the bus? Or does she miss a lot of school?"

You say, "I will check to see if Kaylee goes straight home after school. I will find out if she talks to anyone. Or if she has a crush on any boys at school."

Mia watches to see how people are treating Kaylee. "I'll find out if someone might be bullying her. And, if she has any friends, other than our group."

Layla checks into all the Karate schools around town.

Each of you try to find out as much as you can about Kaylee.

When you all come back together, you will compare notes.

This story continues on pages 114.

Skylee decides to confront her parents.

After Skylee goes home, she continues to seek out information about her possible sister. From her Facebook posts and pictures, Skylee finds her sister Kenna. She knows that her sister has a car. She's going to college and studying dress design. She has a boyfriend, but when she's not away at college, she stays with her parents. Her sister Kenna loves riding horses and going hiking. She says she's not an only child, but she lives like one. Does that mean that she has a sister, but her sister isn't living with the family?

Skylee also loves horses, but she has never ridden a horse, even though she reads books about horses, and collects pictures of horses.

There are no other siblings at the house where Skylee lives. She only has her parents; she loves them and doesn't want to do anything to make them unhappy. They have never mistreated her. They give her what they can, but they don't have much. They may have left everything behind when they kidnapped her. They left their home for sure and possibly left their jobs. Her dad has a degree in nursing and her mom has a degree in robotic engineering. Rather than using their college degrees to get better jobs, her dad works as a janitor and her mom as a waitress at a local diner.

This story continues on page 68.

Skylee goes into their home office and looks at her parent's certificates. "Oh, my gosh! They both graduated from college in Saint Louis! The last name on their degrees doesn't match our last name of Williamson."

In fact, her mom once explained it by saying that her degree certificate had her maiden name and that after college, Skylee's dad took the last name of his stepdad. *Why don't they want to make a better living, after earning a degree?*

Her mom often says, "We could do better, but we gave up everything for you, Baby!"

Skylee decides to talk to her parents about her birth record. She walks into the kitchen while her mom is making dinner. "Mom, when I was little, did we live in Missouri?"

"Oh, honey, why do you ask?"

"Because you and Dad both have degrees from Saint Louis, Missouri on the wall in the study."

"Oh yes, we did go to school in Missouri but that was before you came into the family. We moved shortly after you came along."

"So, if you went to college, why don't you work in the jobs that you were trained in?"

"Oh, dear, why so many questions. You know we love you and will do all we can to take care of you."

"Yes, I know that Mom, but why do you work as a waitress when you're an engineer?"

This story continues on page 69.

"That training was so long ago, and we live in a different area. I would have to go back to school to update my degree."

"So, why don't you?"

"We have you to think about now, we will soon be putting you through college and thinking about your future."

Skylee changes the subject, "So, why don't I have a birth certificate? Everyone in this country has a birth certificate unless they are in this country illegally."

"Oh, dear, we had a birth record for you, but it must have been displaced when we moved here. We can get a copy for you."

"Okay, I will write to Missouri records to get a copy of my birth certificate."

"You don't need to trouble yourself with that! I promise to take care of it for you."

"When Mom?" she whines, "I'm in middle school and soon I will want to drive. I need my birth certificate."

"Okay, I will get that for you. Don't worry. I guess it just slipped my mind, that's all."

Skylee later talks to her father, "Dad, what did I look like when I was born. Was I all wrinkly? Did I have hair?"

"Oh yes, your hair was always so blonde and curly." says Dad.

"But, why don't I have any baby pictures? And where do my grandparents live?"

"I think most of your pictures were lost when we moved here. I will ask your mother to look around for them. We still have boxes downstairs that haven't been unpacked.

Your mother and I were both living in foster care when we met, so no, you don't have grandparents, that we know of."

This story continues on page 77.

"We walked home from that building, leaving his car behind. I didn't know who or what he hit, until I started hearing about a woman carrying groceries in a crosswalk, who was hit by a vehicle the same day and now that woman is in a coma."

Mia continues, "The news people said that the police and the woman's family need information, so anyone who knows what happened should come forward."

"Oh Mia, you are carrying a huge secret! If you tell you think you will be in trouble. If you don't, the woman might die, and someone needs to take responsibility," you say.

"I know," says Mia. "Would I be in trouble? Can I ask someone? My brother Ray could be a murderer!"

Harper says, "We aren't going to tell, but I think you should tell someone. One of your parents, a teacher or your counselor."

"I might," says Mia. "I just need to think about it first."

All the girls talk among themselves.

"This is a heavy secret!" says Layla.

"What should Mia do?" you ask.

"If she keeps the secret and the woman dies, she will know that her brother *is* a murderer." says Skylee.

"If she tells, then that could upset and break up her family, but it's a crime to be involved in a hit and run." says Everly.

This story continues on page 71.

"Mia was not driving the car, so she's not a criminal but she is a witness. She could tell the whole story and help the woman's family know what happened," says Skylee.

"Besides, someone could have seen the car, the driver or they could have seen Mia. She isn't doing anyone any favors by keeping quiet!" says Layla.

Mia returns to the conversation, when Skylee says, "There are a few things that you can do, Mia. You could make an anonymous phone call to the family to tell them what kind of car hit their mother."

"Or call the police, and tell them what happened," you suggest.

Ava says, "She could just call and say there is a car that was involved in an accident and tell them where the car is parked. Then the police can do the rest, they can check for blood on the car and test to see if the blood is from the woman who was injured."

"Yeah!" says Everly, "That way she wouldn't have to be involved with the crime or telling on her brother. They'll trace the car back to her brother without any further involvement from her."

Mia says, "That could work, unless someone saw me riding in the car or saw me with my brother, walking away from the car, behind the vacant building."

"Mia, how long ago did this happen?" you ask.

This story continues on page 86.

One, Paisley isn't a runaway, living at Kaylee's house. Two, they are swapping clothes, but it's going both ways. So, Paisley does have her own outfits.

Skylee is watching to see if Kaylee is really eating both snacks after she goes to the store. She sees Kaylee leaving the store with double hotdogs and drinks, but then she walks through the park and sits down on a bench by a tree. In a few minutes she is met by Paisley, and she hands her one set of snacks. So, Kaylee *is* buying double snacks, but it is Paisley who is eating one set of food.

You still don't know Kaylee's secret, but you all decide that she isn't gaining weight because of eating extra snacks. It could be that by taking the bus, instead of walking to and from school, she is gaining weight due to lack of exercise.

The End 21 & 22

 You have just finished reading about the group's guesses concerning Kaylee's secret, in stories 12 and 13.
It's time to choose a new path and try to figure out a new secret.
You Follow Kaylee. Begin story 14 on **page 117**.

From the news reports, you know you are looking for the room of Sebrina Myers. There are a few news people in the waiting room. You notice that some of the woman's family are standing outside her door.

From across the hallway, you, Mia, and Ava can hear their conversation.

"Did you see mom yet?"

"No, we just got here. How is she doing today?"

"She's no better. There hasn't been any change! I hope they catch the SOB who ran her down!"

Mia gasps! They don't seem to notice her.

One of the women continues, "I can't wait to give him a piece of my mind!"

"Did they find the car yet?"

"No, but a witness is sure that the driver was a guy. The car is a blue compact car.

There might have been a passenger in the front seat of the car, as well."

"Yes, I heard that the passenger may be a young girl. I hope she at least does the right thing here. We need to find out who did this to Mom!"

"I hope Mom will wake up soon!"

After the two women leave, the three of you look through the doorway and see Sebrina Myers lying motionless on her bed.

Ava then guides your tearful friend Mia down the hall toward the elevator.

You are pretty sure Mia has seen and heard enough!

This story continues on page 80.

Skylee bursts into tears, sniffing and sobbing. "I'm so sad and feeling so lonely right now. What will happen to my parents? Will I ever see them again?"

"I'm sorry," says the agent. "I really can't answer that question right now."

You watch as she is taken away by an FBI agent.

The other agents wait outside until her parents arrive at the house. You leave the house and wait outside as well. You watch as Skylee's parents are arrested and taken away in handcuffs.

While in DCFS custody, Skylee is fingerprinted to see if her prints match those of Jamie Kinsley. They are positive that Skylee is the girl who went missing from the grocery store when she was only two years old.

You don't need to look far to find the information you want to know.

There is a lot of news coverage from the state of Missouri and the state where Skylee was found, after being kidnapped. Skylee has even made national news as the girl who went missing eleven years ago.

Skylee is reunited with her birth parents and her older sister. She moves from her home and now lives in Missouri. You keep in touch with your friend Skylee and are invited to come and visit her next summer.

The End 9 & 10

You have just finished reading about Skylee's secret in stories 5 and 6.
It's time to choose a new path and learn a new secret.
Will you choose to learn Mia's Secret next? Begin story 7 on **page 64.**

Skylee has planted the idea into her parent's minds and now she waits. She watches through a crack in the door and listens to her dad talking to her mom. "She knows, Irene. I think she knows!"

"No, that's not possible. We moved away from there when she was little. How could she know. She is concerned about not having a birth certificate. That is something we need to take care of right away. Rosie down the street had a birth certificate made for herself. I will ask her who can make one for someone we know. Don't worry, I won't tell them anything."

"Irene, are you sure we should keep going on like this? The whole thing could really backfire. We could both get arrested and be put in jail. I'm worried Irene."

"Skylee wouldn't turn on us now. She couldn't. We are her parents. The only parents she knows. What would make her ask these questions?"

Skylee's mom goes to the loose floorboard and pulls out the box. "No, everything is still here in this box. Right where we put it."

"Irene, get rid of that box! There is no reason to keep that box any longer. Think of where you can dump the box with its contents and do it soon!"

This story continues on page 78.

"Get the birth certificate, dump the box, pretend like everything is okay and normal. Sure, Irene can handle it all," says Skylee's mom.

Skylee decides that she will go and get the box before her mom gets rid of it. After all, those are really *her* things. They are the only items she has that will connect her to her past.

The next day, when Skylee comes home from school, and her parents aren't home, she goes straight to their room and removes the box.

She brings the box to your house and shows you what she has found. You both handle the blanket.

"Skylee, did you notice the name and birthdate on this blanket?" you ask.

"No, I never really pulled it out before. OMG! The baby blanket has the name Jamie embroidered on it!"

"Look, there's also a birth date and year," you point out.

"The birthday I have celebrated all these years isn't my birthday at all! I celebrate May 25, but according to this blanket, my real birthday is the year before, on November 21."

"So, you're older than you thought. Why would they change your birthdate?" you ask.

This story continues on page 79.

"I don't know," says Skylee. "It was probably changed to make sure I wouldn't have too much in common with the kidnapped girl, Jamie Kinsley."

Skylee calls her parents and asks if she can sleep over at your house. They seem calm on the phone and tell her, "Sure, honey, you can sleep over. We'll see you tomorrow."

The next morning, when she calls her mom, the phone goes to a message saying, "*You have reached a number that is no longer in service. Please check the number and dial again.*"

You go home with Skylee and there is no one there, in fact all their things are gone from the house. Other than Skylee's room and the items that belong to her, the whole house was cleared out.

"When the box came up missing from their secret place, they knew that you found out their secret," you say to Skylee.

Skylee is alarmed and starts sobbing. "Where are they? Where will they go? Will they be arrested? Will I ever see my parents again?"

You and Skylee tell your mom everything that happened. She says that it's best to talk to the police. They may be able to catch Skylee's parents before they get too far.

This story continues on page 82.

When you get outside, it's as if all of you were holding your breath. Mia turns to you, "What if that was my mom in there? What if someone hit her with a car? What if this woman never wakes up?

"I've got to do something, like your minister said. I know I have the information the police need. It is up to me to make things right, as much as I can. I need to do the right thing."

You and Ava return to the house with Mia. You call in some of your other friends for backup. Soon Layla and Skylee arrive. All of you wait with your friend Mia, until her mom gets home.

A car drives up the driveway. Her mom gets out of the car with groceries. Mia can hardly wait for her mom to enter the house.

"Mom, I, we need to talk to you."

"Can you wait a minute for me to put the groceries away?"

Mia looks at you, you imagine she's thinking the same thing as you are. The woman in the hospital, the one her brother ran down in the street, never had a chance to put her groceries away! Tears are streaming down your face, and your other friends are struggling to hold back their tears. Mia can hardly talk when her mom comes into the living room.

This story continues on page 81.

"Mom, I have something really important to tell you."

Her mom looks at Mia, then at you and your other friends. Her heart seems to sink. She sits down and listens to the whole story.

"I have been keeping a secret for Ray. I feel so bad about it. It's making me sick.

Ray and I were going to the store on Tuesday. I think Ray was showing off a little with his driving. He was going too fast, but he also messed around with the car radio. He ran a stop sign and we heard and felt a 'thump!' I knew we hit something. Ray did too. I didn't know if we hit an animal or a person."

Her mom gasps and puts her hands over her ears, bracing herself for what might come next. She slowly removes her hands, and motions for Mia to continue.

"Ray kept going and he hid the car in a field, by an old building. We got out of the car and ran home."

Mia continues; "The car isn't in a shop, Mom. It's still in the field. It was a hit and run accident. I later found out that a lady was hit in a crosswalk. She is unconscious in the hospital."

There isn't a sound in the room, besides Mia's voice, and a few uncontrolled sobs.

This story continues on page 90.

81

The police come to your house to talk to Skylee. Between sobs, she points out a place on the map where she has gone with her parents.

"It's about 100 miles away, along the river. There's a cabin we often rent. They might go there."

She gives an involuntary shiver. "Or maybe they will just go to another city to start over."

Skylee knows her parent's real names from the certificates she has seen on the wall. She also has pictures of them on her phone to show the police.

The next thing to do, besides waiting for her parents to be caught, is to allow the police to contact her birth family. This is so hard, yet so exciting for Skylee. She plans to bring the box with the baby blanket and the news article to the meeting with her birth parents.

Skylee asks you to go with her to the meeting. Her birth parents fly from St. Louis to the city where she now lives, and it feels like she is meeting them for the first time. Her sister Kenna is there, Skylee recognizes her from her online pictures. Her sister also recognizes Skylee from her friend request on Facebook.

"Jamie! You're coming home!" says her sister, running to give her a hug.

"Um, you know me as Jamie, but will you please call me Skylee? It's what I've always been called."

"Okay, I think we can get used to calling you Skylee."

This story continues on page 83.

This is both a happy and a sad reunion. You are happy for Skylee and glad she'll be with a family who loves and misses her, but you are sad that she had to leave the parents she's known for so many years.

You will miss your friend Skylee! This family reunion is possible because of the slumber party at your house when you asked your friends to tell a secret. There are some secrets that should always be kept, while others that are critical need to be told to someone you can trust. You are so glad that Skylee trusted her friends.

The End

You have just finished reading Skylee's story #5.
It's time to choose a new path. Will you choose to read more about Skylee?
Should Skylee Continue to Live with Her Parents? Begin story 6 on **page 36**.
Or will you find out Mia's Secret? Begin story 7 on **pages 64 and 65**.

"What is it?" asks Harper's mom. "Did the girls get into trouble?"

"No, it's nothing like that. The girls are all doing well. We just need to have a talk."

Your mother comes back into the family room where you are having the sleepover and tells all of you about the meeting which is set up for the next day.

The evening after the sleepover, your friends return to your family room to join Harper and her parents.

Before the meeting begins, your mom assures Harper that she's not alone, that she hasn't done anything wrong and that she is strong. She promises to sit with Harper as support and you sit on her other side. If she gets stuck on what to say, each of you agree to assist her.

Harper's parents are puzzled, and her mom asks, "Harper, what's this all about? Is something wrong?"

Your mom assures her that they will soon find out. "We have gathered here tonight because of something dire that Harper needs to talk to you about. It's okay Harper. You can do this."

"Mom, and Dad, please let me talk and don't react until I have finished."

This story continues on page 96.

Mia answers, "Well, um, it happened on Tuesday, and now it's Friday, so it was three days ago."

"Okay, and no one has come forward as a witness yet?" asks Ava.

"No," says Mia.

"If someone had seen you riding with your brother, or knew where he parked the car, then I think they would have said something by now," says Skylee.

What should Mia do? It's time to choose a path.

Should Mia make an anonymous call to the police, reporting the car? Story 7 continues on **page 87**.

Mia Won't Tell on Her Brother. Begin story 8 on **page 26**.

"Okay," says Mia, "I need to do something. If I wait much longer, someone will see the car, or my parents will report it missing. I think I will call the police and make an anonymous report about the car. I'll call from a phone at the community center, just so it can't be traced back to me. Will you all help me do this tomorrow? There will be lots of people around so no one will know who made the call."

"Sure, we will! What are you going to say when you call?"

"Um, I'm going to say that I'm making an anonymous tip. I'll tell them that there is a car parked behind a building that was involved in a hit and run accident. If they pick up the car, they may even find evidence of an accident, where a woman was hit in a crosswalk."

Skylee says, "Okay, that way you will turn in the car, and they will find your brother. You already tried to tell him to stop and to turn himself in, and that didn't work. Mia, you won't even have to tell the police your brother's name. They will figure it out when they find the car."

"Yes, I am a witness, but neither of us really saw what we hit. I won't let my parents, or my brother know that I turned in the car. The police would find it eventually, anyway."

This story continues on page 88.

"Mia, if you do this, you will still have to keep a secret from your brother and your parents. Are you okay with that?"

"Yes, yes, I think I am." she says.

"Hey, I have a better idea," says Ava. "You shouldn't even go to the community center tomorrow. You could just stay home and do whatever you want, but make sure that you're around your family when the call is made. That way your brother can't connect that call to you."

You suggest, "The rest of us could go to the community center and one of us will make the call. Then you won't have to keep the secret from your family. The truth will be that you didn't make the call. You were at home with your family when the call came into the police station."

Mia says, "I like that even better! Would you really do that for me?"

You all nod your heads in agreement.

"If someone else makes the call, the truth would be out, and I will still be at home with my family. Thank you, thank you!"

Mia continues, "I can't have my whole family turn on me for something my brother did. He refused to tell the truth. I'm okay as long as none of you breathe a word of this to anyone. Do you all promise?"

This story continues on page 92.

After your mom is called into the room to talk to Harper about her secret, you speak up, "Mom, if you overheard anything, you need to be sworn to secrecy. We are telling each other our secrets, but agreed to never tell anyone what we share. We don't know what happened to Kaylee because when it was her turn to speak up, she turned red and backed up saying, 'No! I can't tell anyone my secret . . .ever!'"

"I promise not to tell," says Mom. "But. . . sometimes a secret is not meant to be kept. There are some secrets that can hurt someone if you don't speak up!"

Your mom continues, "Let me give you an example: when I was about your age, I saw something I never should have seen, and I kept it a secret. This secret was so awful and so harmful that others were being hurt by it. I finally had to tell someone because I knew it was so horrible and illegal."

You gasp... "What is it, Mom? Do I know about it?"

"No, you don't know about it. But when I was thirteen, I was sleeping over at my neighbor's house. You know my best friend, Jennifer?"

You nod your head. Your mom continues, "Her parents were gone for the evening, and we were playing around."

This story continues on pages 94 and 95

"Mom, today I went to talk to a minister, because he can't tell anyone about something that is told to him in secret. He said to pray and to do the right thing." Motioning to you and Ava, Mia adds, "Next we went to the hospital."

Mia continues, "We heard her family talking in the hallway. Their mom hasn't woken up yet. They knew that the car that hit her was blue, and the witness could tell that a guy was driving. They called Ray a SOB and said there was a younger girl in the car along with the driver. After those two women left, we peeked into the room and saw the woman lying on a bed. She was still breathing but not moving."

Mia's mom who is still listening, stands up, walks around the room, picks up her phone then puts it down again.

"Mom, what if someone hit you with a car? What if you were in a hospital bed and we didn't know who hit you?

"I told Ray to stop. I also told him to turn himself in, but he wouldn't. The police will find the car. They will!"

Mia tells her mom, "We need to turn Ray in. He has committed a crime. I know I'm not guilty, but I am a witness."

Her mom sits back down, silently shaking. With her head in both hands, she looks up and quietly asks, "Who else have you told, Mia? Who else knows about this?"

This story continues on page 91.

"Only a few friends. Most of them are in this room."

"Okay, don't speak about this to anyone else. I am going to talk to my lawyer before I tell the police what happened. We will need good advice."

Mia's mother calls her lawyer before you even get up from the couch. He refers her to a criminal lawyer. When Ray comes home, he is confronted by both parents with the lawyer in the room. He wants Ray to tell him everything, from start to finish. He also talks to Mia, to get her side of the story.

The lawyer lets the family know that there will be criminal charges filed and that Ray could face hefty fines and jail time for the crime of hit and run. They learn that Ray could be charged with a misdemeanor.

Ray is still a minor, but he is only a few months away from his eighteenth birthday.

The lawyer goes with the family to the police station, for Ray to turn himself in.

Mia will be a witness in the court case.

The End 12

You have finished reading about Mia's secret in stories 7 and 8. Now it's time to choose a new path and learn a new secret.

Will you choose to learn Harper's Secret? Begin story 9 on **page 12.**

Will you choose to learn Ava's Secret? Begin story 11 on **page 101.**

"Yes, Mia, I promise."

You all swear not to tell.

"Now I feel much better," says Mia.

Mia is home when her group of friends ride bikes to the community center on Saturday. Layla volunteers to make the phone call.

"Police Department, how may I direct your call?

"Hello, I want to make an anonymous tip".

"Hold on one second while I transfer your call to the tip line."

Someone else comes on the phone. "This is the tip line. How may I help you?"

"I want to make an anonymous tip."

"Okay, did you witness a crime, or do you have information that will help solve a crime?"

"Yes, says Layla. "I have information that will help to solve a crime."

"Okay, and you say you want the tip to be anonymous?"

"Yes, if it's not anonymous than I can't leave my tip."

"Okay. Please state your tip."

"I have information concerning the hit and run accident on Tuesday night, involving a woman who was hit by a car in a crosswalk."

This story continues on page 93.

"Okay," the officer repeats back to Layla what she just said. "You say you have information concerning the hit and run accident involving a woman who was hit in a crosswalk?"

"Yes, that's right. There is a car parked behind an abandoned building near Segway and Alameda. The building is at the front of a large field. I think that if you pick up the car, you may find blood on the front fender. This will lead to the suspect involved with the accident."

She repeats Layla's words back to her. "You are reporting an abandoned car behind a building near Segway and Alameda. The car may contain blood from a hit and run victim? Is that correct Ma'am?

"Yes, that's right."

"Would you be willing to be a witness in this case if it goes to court?"

"No, I did not witness the accident."

"Okay, thank you for your tip!"

Layla hangs up and you all hug her and give a sigh of relief.

You text Mia to let her know that the call was made. You also suggest that she should delete this message, as a precaution, so no one will see it on her phone.

This story continues on page 98.

Your mom continues. "I hid from Jennifer, and I was going to jump out and scare her. I was hiding in her dad's office when something caught my eye. There were large pictures on his desk, mostly covered by a pile of books, but a corner was visible. I pulled them out because I wondered if they were pictures of my friend when she was younger, but they weren't."

She continues, "in these pictures, there were children; both boys and girls undressed and in provocative poses. This was horrible! I didn't know who the children were, but I knew that this was so wrong!"

"I didn't know why my neighbor had these pictures. But what I did know was that this was an awful, terrible secret. It was me who felt guilty! I felt dirty."

"Mom, what did you do?"

"I made an excuse to go home. I didn't tell Jennifer the truth. And then I had to live with it. I closed my eyes at night, and I saw these pictures. I felt that what I saw would never leave the inside of my eyes. This went on for several weeks. I changed inside because of what I saw.

I became withdrawn. I wouldn't talk to my parents, and I wouldn't talk at school. I didn't leave my room on weekends. My parents thought something bad had happened, but they didn't know what."

This story continues on page 102.

Harper continues, "I have a favorite cousin, Jada. You know how close we are. Well, when I was ten, I was sleeping over at Jada's house and her father, Uncle Paul... touched me inappropriately. He also tried to kiss me, like a man kisses a woman."

"What, Harper? Do you know what you're saying?" asks her dad, standing up suddenly.

"Yes, Dad. I do know what I'm saying. It's true. I haven't told anyone because everyone loves Uncle Paul."

Her mother comes over and asks to sit next to her daughter. You move to another seat, allowing her to have your chair. She puts her arm around Harper's shoulder. Both Harper and her mom are sobbing now.

Her dad says, "Don't you feel stupid saying such things that aren't true? Uncle Paul is my brother. Why would you accuse him of such things?"

Harper continues with a shaky voice. "It's true, Dad. How could your beloved brother do those things to a child?"

Harper says, "I didn't tell anyone before, but I wouldn't sleep over at their house after that. Jada always had to come to our house."

Harper is not making eye contact with anyone, but she manages to continue speaking. "This didn't happen again until last Christmas."

This story continues on page 97.

Harper continues, "We had a Christmas party at our house and I needed to go to the bathroom. Uncle Paul must have seen me leave the room. He followed me into the bathroom, and he touched me and tried to kiss me again. He really did touch me! I'm older now and he touched me under my blouse. I ran out of the bathroom and went outside to get some air, before returning to the family room."

Now her dad is sobbing, both for his daughter and for his brother.

"The reason I'm telling this now is because I'm worried that Jada might be molested by her own dad. I also have younger cousins, Deja and Nia. I'm worried about what Uncle Paul might do to them if he isn't stopped!"

Your mom speaks up. "When my daughter suggested that Harper should talk to me, I suggested a meeting with her parents," she sweeps her arm around the room, including them in her motion. "We are all here to help Harper get through this, but if you want me to back out, I certainly will."

Your mom continues, "I work at a law office, and I do know some things involving the law. I would say that, obviously, this criminal act wasn't a one-time incident. Legally if you talk to a minister, a lawyer, or a doctor about this, they will keep what is said in confidence. A counselor will be obligated to speak up about what is told unless they are a Doctor of Psychology.

"May I make a suggestion?" your mother asks.

This story continues on page 108.

You all ride bikes back to your house before deciding what to do next.

Skylee suggests, "Let's ride our bikes to see the car, near the abandoned building. That way we can get a look at the car and see if any cop's show up to tow away the wreaked vehicle."

When your group arrives at Segway and Alameda streets, the car is there, right where Mia said it would be. It is partly hidden in the weeds and rubbish surrounding the building. Your group examines the front of the car, being careful not to touch anything. There is damage, like Mia said, with blood on the bumper.

You notice a patrol car, going slowly down the street so all of you get back on your bikes and head in the opposite direction.

The only thing to do is wait for Mia to text you about the cops showing up at her house.

It isn't until the next day when you get a string of frantic texts from Mia.

"It happened just the way you said. The cops found the car, which was registered to my parents. They came to my house to talk to my mom and dad, asking about the wrecked car. My parents told them that my brother was driving that car, but he'd told them that it was in the shop being repaired."

This story continues on page 99.

"The cops said that the car was not taken to a garage for repairs. It had been involved in a hit and run accident where a woman was hurt. She is in the hospital in critical condition."

"The police spoke to my brother. At first, he said he didn't do it. But then he confessed. He knew he hit something, but he didn't know he hit a person. Ray said he didn't stop to find out, he just kept going."

"Now I might be in trouble too, because my brother said that I was in the car with him. I hope I'm not in trouble!"

Later you find out that Mia is not in trouble for the accident, after all.

She and her brother were questioned separately. Mia told the police that she tried to get her brother to stop at the scene of the accident. She tried to get Ray to turn himself in, but he wouldn't.

Her brother backed up her story, telling the officer that his sister told him to stop, but he didn't stop at the scene of the accident. He just kept driving and went to a field and hid the car behind an abandoned building.

Mia's brother Ray is taken into custody.

Since Mia is an eyewitness, she could be asked to testify in court for an insurance company or by the victim's family.

This story continues on page 100.

KEEPING SECRETS: THE PATH YOU CHOOSE #4

You are so glad that Mia isn't in trouble. And Mia is relieved that she had a chance to tell her side of the story. If Mia hadn't confided in you and your group of friends, it would have taken longer for this problem to be solved by the police and the victim's family would have suffered longer, not knowing what happened to their mother.

The End 11

You have just finished reading story #7 which is Mia's secret. It's time to choose a new path: Will you continue reading about Mia?

Mia's Won't Tell On Her Brother in story 8, turn to **page 26**.

Ava is quiet while the others are taking their turn talking about their secrets. She hardly moves, but you can tell she is crying.

When it's her turn to speak up, she says, "I'm worried about Layla because if she tells her dad about her mom cheating, then she will break up her family. I was ten when my parents divorced, and every day I wish they would get back together. My mom moved away. She took my little sister and my brother to live with her and I was stuck living with my dad and my stepmom. I have an older sister too, but she's never home. She doesn't spend much time with me or my dad. It's just us!"

Everyone is worried about Ava. Layla has her head in her hands.

Finally, Layla speaks up, "I know things will also get bad for me, since I found out that my mom is cheating!"

"I get it, Layla. I spend time with my mom in the summer, but the thing is that my younger brother and sister spend time with my dad at the same time, while I'm gone. So, I never get to see them. I'm alone. I'm always lonely and there are things that girls just can't talk to their dads about. My stepmom works a lot, and she hangs out with my dad or her friends on weekends. She helps me with homework occasionally and she does cook dinner a few times a week, but I'm not important to her. She mostly just ignores me."

This story continues on page 116.

"What did you do?" asks Layla. "Did you ever tell?"

"Yes. I was in my health class, and they were talking about the effect sexual abuse has on children, when I burst into tears. I was sobbing and had to be taken to the office."

She continues, ". . . I couldn't talk. I couldn't eat. I couldn't sleep. My parents thought I was on drugs. I was so depressed that I was taken to a mental hospital. That was where I finally got some help. A dirty secret was literally eating me alive. I had to tell someone. I finally did tell a counselor at the hospital. She got me to talk about it. This was weeks, or probably months after I saw the pictures.

The thing is, this was so bad that the counselor had to report it to the authorities. The sheriff came to talk to me. He told me that if I didn't tell him where I saw the pictures, the children in the pictures would continue to suffer, and they might never recover. If the pictures were affecting me this way, then what about those children?"

"What happened next, Mom?"

"I told them about Jennifer's dad. Right after that, undercover officers were set up to watch my neighbor and watch his house. They also had to find out who he was meeting with and where he was going in his free time."

This story continues on page 103.

Mom continues, "After they gathered evidence, they not only arrested my neighbor's dad, but also the whole ring of child pornographers.

Because I told my secret, the authorities were able to find out who the children were, and they arrested some of their parents as well as taking the children into protective custody. The children were taken to a safe place, where they could also receive therapy."

Mom continues, "This all happened because I was hiding in my neighbor's office, saw some pictures and finally told someone what I saw. Since I hadn't told Jennifer or her mom what I had seen, they weren't able to tip him off and he wasn't able to get anything out of the house before the officers showed up at his door. He was caught with not only those pictures, but also video tapes of the same type as the pictures I'd seen.

That was back when there were video tapes and when there wasn't so much going on with the internet."

"So, Mom," you interrupt, ". . . did he go to jail after that?"

"Yes, he was arrested many years ago. When or if he gets out, he will be labeled as a sex offender. You have never met him, and if I can help it, you never will."

This story continues on page 106.

"I was supposed to follow you to see where you were going at night. I would then keep the record of where you went. You didn't go out at night, so I switched to following you in the daytime.

"OMG!" says Kaylee.

"I saw you getting on a bus, so I followed, boarding the bus as well. You then took a second bus to Brennon St."

Kaylee swallows hard, then tears are streaming down her face.

You continue, "I followed you to a house where you watched a couple of young girls on bikes, and then the mom said she wanted to have the girls come in and get ready to go on some errands and then go to a horse ranch."

Kaylee gasps! "You followed me? You saw where I went then? No, you got that wrong! I did go there, but that's not why. The reason, if you must know, is so much different than you can imagine. So much more than I could have ever imagined. It won't be a secret for long anyway, because soon everyone will be talking about the pregnant fourteen-year-old."

You are stunned for a moment, but you also care about your friend. You run to put your arms around Kaylee. "Are you okay?"

"Yes, I'm okay now. I told my sister Sharon, and I also told my mom."

This story continues on page 110.

It's Friday night and you have nothing better to do, so you spend several hours watching outside Kaylee's house, but she doesn't go out. You go home and decide on another tactic. You go back on Saturday when it's light outside. You wait on the other side of a fence, near Kaylee's house.

Kaylee leaves the house, and she's walking down the street. You follow her at a safe distance. She stops and waits for a city bus, on the corner. You also wait for the bus, but she doesn't notice you.

She gets on the bus, and you also get on, with a hood pulled down low so she can't see who you are.

Kaylee has a paper that she keeps looking at. She gets off the bus and then quickly crosses the street to wait for a second bus.

You also leave the bus, cross the street, and stand back to wait. This time you get on the bus ahead of Kaylee. When she gets on the second bus, she asks the bus driver, "Will you let me know where I should get off to go to Brennon St.?"

"Sure, it will be the fifth light and you will need to go to the right, after that light."

"Okay, thanks."

You are getting nervous that Kaylee will see you. If she gets off at the front of the bus, you will get off at the back.

This story continues on pages 118 and 119.

"What happened to your friend Jennifer and her mom?"

"They sold their house and moved to Chicago to live with Jennifer's grandparents. My friend Jennifer is living in Maryland now. She wasn't directly affected by what her father did, except that her whole life was turned upside down. She now has a good job working in Washington, DC. I still keep in touch with her sometimes.

And so, girls, my point is that a secret and maybe even a promise can't always be kept. Keeping that secret or making a promise to keep someone else's secret can sometimes be very dangerous and harmful. You need to decide when to keep secrets and when you really need to tell someone."

"Thank you, Mom. I had no idea that you went through that! I'm so glad you finally told your secret and got help."

"Me too, baby! Me too!"

The End 15
You have just finished reading about your mom's secret in story # 10.
It's time to choose another path and learn about another secret.

Will you choose to learn Ava's Secret? Begin story 11 on **page 101.**

Will you choose to learn Harper's Guess about what Kaylee's secret might be. Begin story 13 on **page 23.**

Mia says, "No, we don't but we know that Kaylee is going somewhere at night, when she says she's sleeping over at my house. But she didn't come to my house, so I know she's lying."

"Okay, so she's lying about her whereabouts. How do you know it's Karate lessons, then?"

"That's on me," says Layla. "I thought it must be Karate lessons because she's gaining weight and she wants to defend herself against the bullies."

"Okay, girls. I can't go along with your imaginations here. I will need proof. I *will* look into whether Kaylee is being bullied, though. I want all my students to feel safe at this school."

When he stands up from his desk you know the meeting is over. "We will talk again when we have something more substantial to go on. Thank you for sharing your concerns."

You shake your head, wondering why the principal didn't believe anything your group just told him in confidence.

When you all meet up the next day after school, Harper says, "I followed Kaylee around and I watched her eating a normal lunch at school. She had two tacos, a small serving of apple sauce and milk. There is nothing unusual about that."

This story continues on page 120.

Harper's mom says, "Yes, please."

Your mom continues, "I suggest that you contact Jada to see if she has been touched by her father. Then hire a lawyer going forward, even if it's only for advice."

The others in the room are momentarily silent. Harper's mom is the first to speak. "I for one believe Harper. I know he's your brother, Jamal. He's my brother-in-law. We spend holidays together; we have been on vacations together. But Harper is our daughter; we are obligated to protect her. She is the victim here and your brother needs to be stopped.

Jamal, if you want to believe your brother over your daughter, I will get in touch with our lawyer and follow through with this crazy fiasco and get to the bottom of this. I will not allow one person, who can't control themselves, ruin the life of my daughter or the lives of any of my nieces. Either you are in, or you are out, but I'm in." She hugs her daughter and tells her, "You are so brave!"

She continues, "I'm not going to confront my sister-in-law, Marlene or Jada until I get good advice from my lawyer."

After that, Harper's father, Jamal gets up, shakes his head at Harper and her mom and leaves the house.

"I'm sorry about him," Harper's mom says to you and your mom.

"I think we should go to a hotel room for tonight," she says to Harper.

This story continues on page 109.

"No, no. You should both stay here. I insist!" says your mom.

You say, "Yes, we have plenty of room!"

Your dad goes with Harper and her mother to get a few things from their house, since her father is not being cooperative.

On Monday, Harper's mom contacts her lawyer. The lawyer recommends a child abuse lawyer that he knows. The new lawyer lets them know, "There are two kinds of cases. One is a civil case where the victim will settle for money to cover damages done to them or to pay for counseling."

He continues, "In a civil case, there is nothing to stop the perpetrator from continuing to abuse children.

"The other kind of case is a criminal case. This case can be tried in court with a jury, but most of these cases are settled outside court. In this case, if the perpetrator is found guilty, he can serve some time in prison, and he will be labeled a sex offender for the rest of his life.

In a criminal case, the victim may be asked to give testimony of what happened at the hands of the perpetrator. In some cases, the testimony can be recorded, so you won't need to be in the courtroom to face your uncle. You, as the victim should have been safe with your uncle, and he was trusted by family members."

This story continues on page 111.

"My sister took me to the police department, and we filled out a report because I was dating an older guy that I met on the internet. He is married and lied about his age."

She takes out her phone and shows you, his picture.

"Wait a minute, Kaylee. Is this the family you went on the bus to see?"

"Yes."

"Kaylee, how old did this guy say he is?"

"He told me he was twenty, but he's really 43! No wonder you thought he was my dad!"

She pulls up his profile on Facebook. "I found him on Facebook a few weeks ago, and he is married with a family. He used his real name, Nick, but a different last name. I even looked up his wife, and she owns a horse ranch."

"Oh, now this whole thing makes more sense. You dated a guy who said he was twenty? Then you found out that he is married with a family. Kids that are already in school. That's why you went to the house that day!"

"Yes, I found him, and you followed me."

"I also understand why you were crying. He said he was your boyfriend, and now you are having a baby. His baby. But you found out he is married."

This story continues on page 144.

The lawyer also tells them, "There will need to be proof. This proof may come because of the testimony of others, saying that they too have been molested, or from a parent who noticed a change in the child that took place around the time of the abuse. The evidence, in Harper's case, can be that she refused to sleep over with her cousin, after the abuse, and only saw her cousin for sleepovers at her own home.

"Child Protective Services will need to be involved, since Harper is a minor. Harper also has a reasonable fear that her uncle may have molested her cousin Jada. She is also afraid that he may have or still may abuse her younger cousins, Deja, and Nia."

Harper isn't looking for money from her uncle for the things he has done, so she decides that they will go for the criminal charges. The report comes back from the CPS worker after she talks to Jada and her mom. The protective service worker also talks to Deja, Nia, and their mother.

This story continues on page 112.

You talk to Harper the next day, she tells you, "Jada and her mother knew that Uncle Paul was a pervert!"

She says, "He has tried to do the same things to his own daughter, ever since Jada was five. When Jada was ten, she told her mother, who is my aunt. Her mother threatened him that if he ever touched her again, she would ruin his life and he would go to prison. Jada said he never did it again. She didn't know that he did it to me, but she says she knows now, and she believes me. Her mother Marlene knew that it happened to her daughter, so she also believes me. The family secret has finally come out and now, something can be done to stop it."

Harper continues, "A woman from family services talked to Deja and Nia, along with their mother. Nia, who is seven years old, told her about a few times when Uncle Paul touched her and kissed her.

"A police report has been filed and Uncle Paul has been arrested. He will be held in jail until his trial, and I have a choice in whether to testify in court. The DA has all the recorded testimonies. My uncle can either plead guilty or not guilty; if he pleads guilty, there won't be a trial. If not, Uncle Paul will be shamed even further before the judge and jury. There is no way out for him now."

This story continues on page 113.

Harper says, "My dad told me he is so sorry for doubting me. He knows now that it wasn't easy for me to speak up about this situation and he is so sad about his brother, who should have been a trusted family member. He is even more sad for me and my cousins. He says it's going to be hard for Jada's family, because he knows his brother will go to jail."

The End 13 &14

You have just finished reading about Harper's secret in story 9. It's time to choose a new path and learn another secret.

Will you choose to read about Your Mom's Secret?

Begin story 10 on **page 89.**

To read What is Kaylee Hiding, begin story 12 on **page 16.**

Then together, you will decide if Kaylee is on steroids, if she has a bully, is she taking Karate classes or is there a different secret that none of you have thought about yet.

Your group is convinced that you know Kaylee's secret and that she is being bullied at school. On the following Monday, you all meet outside the principal's office.

When he agrees to see your group, you begin by saying, "We are worried about our friend Kaylee. We think she has someone bullying her at school."

"Girls, I appreciate your concerns for your friend. Do you have any proof that this is going on?"

Mia speaks up, "I was walking by her locker and when she opened it, a group of girls came up behind her and slammed it shut."

"Well, do you know who the girls were?"

"Yes, it was Christy and Becky from the basketball team. I also saw one of the girls take one of her shoes and run off with it before practice last week."

"We think that Kaylee is taking secret Karate lessons so she can get even with the bullies." Says Layla.

You blurt out, "And we think she's taking steroids so she can be stronger and hurt someone who is bullying her."

"Girls, do you have any evidence of any of these things?"

This story continues on page 107.

She continues, lacking emotion, ". . .see, I should have never told any of this to you guys. It's not your fault or your problem.

I really don't want to do it, but I can't live this way either. What do you guys think I should do?"

"Ava," says Mia, "We are your friends. You aren't alone. You always have us to talk to. We do want you to be happy though."

You say, "I think you should talk to your grandparents. If they would let you stay with them, then at least you wouldn't feel so lonely. Even if you go there, you can still visit with us some weekends or holidays when you come to see your dad."

Layla says, "If you feel at home with your grandparents, then that is where you should go. I'm very worried that you feel this way. If you are having suicidal thoughts, then you do need to talk to someone. It needs to be an adult. If you can't talk to your parents alone, I can come with you. Or you can talk to someone you feel close to. Who are you comfortable talking to, Ava?"

Ava says, "Well, my grandma, I think. If I talk to her, she will help me talk to my dad about it."

"I think kids can decide where they want to live when they are over thirteen. Do you think your dad would agree to let you go live with your grandparents?" you ask.

This story continues on page 121.

When she gets off, you follow and she stops and stands behind a tree, outside a house with a manicured lawn.

She stands there and watches while two young children play outside,

riding bikes up and down the street. Kaylee isn't talking to anyone. She just watches.

You are waiting and watching the house from the side of a neighbor's garage. You hope no one notices you.

Soon a woman comes outside and says to the girls, "You need to put the bikes up and get ready to go. We need to do some errands before going out to the horse ranch."

"Mommy, do we get to ride horses today?" asks one of the girls.

"Yes, honey we can ride horses!"

"Oh goody. I get to ride my horse, Cody!" She runs toward the front door.

Mom yells, "Grab a change of clothes because you will probably get dirty."

You are standing several feet away, but you think Kaylee may be crying.

Kaylee seems to be standing there, frozen.

The dad drives up in front of the house. The girls run out and throw their arms around his neck. "Daddy, Daddy!"

The wife tells him that they are going to the horse ranch.

This story continues on page 128.

"No, I agree that's not overeating." Skylee says, "I followed Kaylee, and she caught the bus to school. But then she walked home after basketball practice."

"Okay, again, not unusual. Did anyone bully her at practice?" asks Mia.

Skylee says, "One of her teammates took her backpack and chased around with it for a while, Kaylee was yelling at her, but she soon returned the backpack to Kaylee."

You say, "I checked to see if Kaylee went straight home after school. She did, like Skylee said. She walked home after practice. I saw her enter her house. No one else was around. I didn't see a bully outside her house or anything."

"Okay, Layla, did you check with the Karate schools in this area?"

Layla looks up in surprise. "Oh, yeah. I called several schools for Karate. They all end at 7:00 or 8:00 at night and no one has classes in the middle of the night. I also checked to see if Kaylee was registered with any of the Karate schools as a student or if she's a teacher at the schools. She's not."

Ava says, "Hey guys! I really don't think this is Kaylee's secret. It was a good guess, but it just didn't check out."

Footnotes 18, 19 & 20

What happens next is up to you! It's time to choose a path.

To learn Harper's Guess about Kaylee's secret? begin story 13 on **page 23.**

You Follow Kaylee. Begin story 14 on **page 105.**

"I... I don't know. But I do need to change something. These feelings may take over in a bad way."

"Okay, Ava, make us a promise that you will talk to your grandma and that you won't do anything to hurt yourself. Promise, Ava!" demands Skylee.

"Okay, okay. I won't hurt myself. But I don't think I should go home this weekend. Can I stay with you for a few days?" she asks you.

"Yes, that's a good start. While you are here, we are going to talk to your grandma. You can let her talk to your dad for you, so it won't be so awkward. You are going to get through this, Ava! I will do anything I can to help!"

Mia, Skylee, Everly, Layla, and Harper all say they will help Ava as well. Ava gets permission to stay with you for the rest of the weekend. She makes a call to her grandmother. You hear both sides of the conversation.

"Grandma, I really miss you!" says Ava.

"Oh, honey. I miss you too!"

"I'm unhappy, Grandma. I don't feel at home with my dad because he's working and doesn't understand girls. My sister is always gone, and I never see my mom, even when I stay with her during the summer."

This story continues on page 122.

"That sounds so hard, honey," her grandmother says, sounding concerned.

"Yes, I'm so lonely here that I feel like I'm either going to run away or commit suicide," Ava adds. "...I'm afraid, Grandma. I really want to live with you because I feel at home when I'm with you."

"Oh, honey! Please don't do anything drastic. I can see how upset you are. I know your dad loves you!"

"I know he does, Grandma. I just need to stay with you. Please!"

"I will have to talk with your dad about this. If he agrees, you can certainly come and live with us, Ava."

"Oh, thank you, Grandma!"

"Hang in there, Ava! Grandpa and I will come to town next week. I think we can get there by Wednesday. Then we can all sit down and have a talk about this."

"Oh, I can hardly wait! Yes, I will see you then."

Ava stays with you over the weekend, and later the next week, Ava, her dad, grandparents, and her sister sit down to talk about her situation. Her grandparents are concerned with her mental health and want her to see a counselor before anything else is decided.

Ava sees a counselor the following day. She is evaluated and told that she's suffering from depression.

This story continues on page 123.

Her family and the counselor talk about her suicidal thoughts and agree that she should go into treatment at a hospital to make sure that her mood is stable.

"For one thing," the counselor points out to Ava and her family, "We need to treat the problem. If Ava moves away to live with her grandparents, it may help for a short time, but the depression will still be there."

Ava agrees to being treated at a hospital. She is put on medication to help with her depression.

During a family group session at the hospital, a therapist tells Ava's family that, "...there are underlying problems causing suicidal feelings and being lonely isn't the only problem here. Ava is still upset with the breakup of her family. She hasn't dealt with her mom leaving her when she was ten, that her older sister rarely speaks to her, and that her younger siblings are no longer around."

With the encouragement of the therapist, Ava shared, "I'm also upset that my mother won't even take some time off when I visit her in the summer. She leaves me alone in the house while she works. I also wish for time with my younger siblings. I wish for time with my dad, doing things that dads do with their daughters, such as fishing, taking a boat out on the lake or going out for ice cream."

This story continues on page 126.

After talking to her sister Sharon and telling her mom what happened, Kaylee finally feels like she can talk to her friends about her secret. She comes to your house to talk to you.

"I'm so sorry that I ran out of your house when you asked me to tell my secret. I just couldn't. Not that you aren't my best friends.

I am ready to tell you now."

"Kaylee, let me first tell you that we *are* your friends. We wanted to help so we have been following you around, making sure you are okay, and well, trying to guess your secret."

"You have?"

"Yes, and I want to tell you what your group of friends has come up with, so you can tell us if we came close."

"Harper and Skylee said that you were going out at night, and they came up with a guess that you had a runaway girl, Paisley, sleeping under your bed or in the closet. They figured that you were going out at night, with Paisley and tagging. That was because you both like to do artwork."

"What?" says Kaylee. "You really thought that? It's so far off and sounds so crazy!"

"I know now. They also said you were going to 7-11 and coming back with extra snacks. That was just a guess, until Skylee watched you come out of the 7-11."

This story continues on page 134 and 135.

Her dad says, "I will try to do better. I think the problem was that Ava reminded me too much of her mother, and that made me feel sad. So, I guess in the beginning I would isolate myself from her, rather than being around for daddy daughter outings.

Now that I'm remarried, I have a new wife to think about and I didn't realize that I'm still self-isolating, out of habit."

Her sister Abby says, "I don't have a family, since my parents split up. I don't talk to Ava because she is younger, and we have nothing in common and nothing to talk about."

Her mother is not in the room but speaks from a video chat room.

"Since I'm raising a family alone, I must work hard to support them in the lifestyle they are used to. I also keep working more than needed because it's the way I cope with things. When my little ones are gone with their dad for the summer, I don't have to pay for daycare."

Her mom continues, "That's why I work even more hours to catch up on expenses. I just figured that Ava was old enough to stay alone without supervision.

"I now realize that I was wrong. I didn't think about what it was doing to my darling daughter. I am so sorry for not putting you first, Ava!"

This story continues on page 127.

When Ava is stable with her treatment, and ready to leave the facility, she is given the choice of where to live.

"I want to stay with my grandparents," she says to the counselor.

Before moving in with her grandparents, they set up an appointment with a therapist in their area, so Ava will have someone to follow-up with her treatment.

After Ava moves, she is happy living with her grandparents, and you even visit her out of town, sometimes.

Arrangements are made with her dad so she can visit him every other weekend. On her dad's weekends Ava often goes on short trips with her father and her older sister.

One weekend, her dad takes them to a cabin to go fishing. He tells her and her sister about the things he did when he was younger, such as sleeping out under the stars. Talking to her dad and sister also helps her and her family to heal.

On many of the trips, they each get to bring a friend. Ava brings you on a river rafting trip and her sister brings her boyfriend along.

Ava's mother even comes to Ava's counseling sessions sometimes.

This story continues on page 147.

"Just give me a minute to change clothes, and I will go with you."

What is Kaylee doing? Why is she watching this family and crying? Is this her real dad? Is he ignoring Kaylee because he now has a new family?

Should you ask Kaylee?

Would it be best if you just forget about it and let Kaylee deal with her own situation?

Kaylee stands there and watches until they all come out of the house. The man and woman hug briefly, and she tells him, "I'm so glad you came home in time, Nick. This will be a great day at the ranch with our family."

"Thank you, Michelle! I can hardly wait!"

Kaylee watches while the car is backing out of the driveway. She then slowly turns around and walks back toward the bus stop.

What happens next is up to you! It's time to choose a path.

Should you speak to Kaylee on the bus about her secret?

Continue story 14 part 1 on **page 129.**

You Think You Know Kaylee's Secret, begins with story 14 part 2 on **page 130.**

You have followed Kaylee on the bus to a house where she was watching a family. You suspect that the man you saw was her father who had left her when she was younger, but you can't be sure without talking to her. You find Kaylee at the bus stop, waiting for a bus to go home.

"Hi Kaylee, are you okay?"

"Oh, hi. What are you doing here?" she asks.

"I was about to catch a bus, but I saw that you were also waiting for the same bus."

You followed her there, but you are hoping she won't ask because it would be hard for you to explain.

"I... I'm fine. I just had an upsetting day," says Kaylee.

"People aren't always the way you think they are," she says.

Let me tell you what happened to me. Maybe it will help if I talk to someone."

"Okay, Kaylee. The whole group is sad for you. We know you must be living with a hard secret. Is there anything we can do to help?"

She seems to have changed her mind now. "I'm sorry.

You really can't help me. No one can right now."

This story continues on page 137.

You think you know Kaylee's secret

When you report to the group about following Kaylee on Saturday, you tell your other friends that you know that Kaylee is not going out tagging on weekends. At least, that's not what you saw.

"Wait until you hear this. I think I know Kaylee's secret." You tell the group that you followed Kaylee to a house on Brennon Street. "She just stood outside the house, a little way off. She was watching two little girls playing outside on their bikes. Then the mom came out of the house.

She didn't look anything like Kaylee, so she wasn't related, unless. . ."

"What is it?" asks Mia.

"Well, the mom told the girls to get ready because they were going to run some errands before going to the horse ranch. Then the dad drove up and the girls hugged him and kissed him. The mom told him where they were going, and he decided to go with them."

You continue, ". . . when they next came out of the house, the mom was hugging the dad and saying how nice it was to have him home and that she was happy he was going with them, and they were going to have a great day at the horse ranch, with the family.

But this is what I want to tell you. Kaylee was crying. She didn't talk to them or say anything. After the car left the driveway, Kaylee just turned around and headed back to the bus stop."

This story continues on page 132.

Kaylee goes to the slumber party because she wants to hang out with her friends. The girls are playing a game where each girl tells a personal secret, but everyone in the room promises not to tell. When they talk about cute boys, they have a crush on, it makes Kaylee very uncomfortable.

She knows that the only boy she has a crush on isn't even a boy. When they met online, Nick told her that he was twenty, but now she suspects he might be thirty.

She found his Facebook profile by searching for a "Nick" living in the city where she lives.

He said his name was Nick Carpenter, but that name didn't come up in an online search. Then when she just searched for "Nick." She found him. It was his picture: his first name was the same—Nick. But his last name was Roberts.

Why would he lie to her? She didn't know. He told her he loved her, was that also a lie?

The profile she found had him working as an engineer for the city.

The Nick that Kaylee thought she knew, lives in a middle-class neighborhood with a wife and a couple of kids!

The girls, his daughters, looked like they were school age.

This story continues on page 133.

"Did Kaylee see you?" asks Mia.

"No, whatever she's dealing with, she wasn't even looking around, and she didn't see me. She just waited for her bus and headed home. I also got on the same busses she did and came home too, without talking to her."

Harper says, "The story has changed. I don't think Kaylee's secret involves hiding a runaway under her bed."

The girls begin to brainstorm about a different secret.

"I think Kaylee was adopted," says Skylee. "This is her birth family and after giving her up at birth, they had more kids, two daughters, and they kept them, giving them everything they wanted. They had bikes and they were heading to a horse ranch, to ride horses."

Everly perks up and says, "I think Kaylee wanted to see what she was missing out on, and she didn't want to talk to them, because it was too painful. What if she had confronted them and they told her they didn't want her, or that she wasn't welcome to visit them?"

You agree that it's what could have happened, but you also suggest, "The next possible secret could be Kaylee's dad left her when she was little. He didn't pay child support and he didn't visit her. In fact, she just barely found out where he lives. She was crying because he now had two younger daughters and he loves them. I saw the girls hug him around the neck. So, Kaylee was sad because he gave these two girls more love than he ever gave her."

This story continues on page 136.

The last time she looked at his profile, he had posted pictures of the kids going to their first day of school. The oldest girl, Hailey was starting third grade and his youngest, Haven started kindergarten.

Kaylee studied his profile and then went to his wife's Facebook page. She's pretty. She's a Sunday school teacher, takes yoga classes and drives the carpool. But what's interesting about her is that she's a lawyer. She doesn't need to work as a lawyer because she inherited a horse ranch and a breeding business. They even own a successful racehorse. Her profile said that she is married, so Kaylee looked for wedding pictures.

All *her* wedding pictures have *Nick* in them.

Kaylee thought he was *her* Nick. The guy who promised her the world. But all he really did was to take the world away from Kaylee.

He took her, a middle school student, and made her pregnant. Nick promised her a world of love and devotion that wasn't *his* to give.

Now Kaylee has nothing. She has no one. How can she tell anyone this secret? How can she?

At the slumber party, Kaylee thinks she might tell her secret, but as the time comes for her to tell, she can't.

This story continues on pages 138 and 139.

She followed you to the park and said that you met Paisley on a park bench, where you shared your snacks with her. Oh, and we also found out that Paisley wasn't staying at your house."

Kaylee says, "No, that's not my secret, but it is funny!"

Then you say, "Here's the next guess. You are being bullied at school, that's why you are taking secret Karate classes so you can fight off your bully. You are also taking steroids to help you get stronger."

"Ha, ha! That's a good one!"

"We care so much about you that we even went to tell the principal and reported that you were being bullied. But we found out that you aren't taking Karate and you aren't doing steroids."

"Oh Wow! that's a stretch!" says Kaylee.

"I think you have a dad who left you when you were young and now, he has a new family."

Kaylee's mouth drops open.

You continue, "But Skylee and Everly think you were given up for adoption and now you have found your birth parents, but they don't claim you."

Kaylee jumps to her feet. "How? Where did you get those ideas? What do you know anyway?"

This story continues on page 104.

Ava says, "I don't know why she didn't go up and talk to her dad and new stepmom. Instead, you say, she just got on the bus, crying and went home."

Without talking to Kaylee, you may never know about her true secret, but because of what you saw when you followed Kaylee across town, everyone agrees that you are close to learning Kaylee's secret, and you all think it must be one of the two scenarios that was decided during brainstorming today.

You know for sure that Kaylee doesn't have a secret runaway hiding under her bed. And that her secret is not about taking Karate lessons or popping steroids so she can get stronger to fight her bully.

The End 23

You have followed Kaylee and now you think you know her secret from stories 14 part 1 and 14 part 2.
It's time to choose a new path and hopefully learn a new secret.
What Is Kaylee's Secret? Begin story 15 on **page 131.**

Kaylee says, "I can't even let you know I'm okay because I don't think I am. It's been hard, very hard. I promise I will talk to you about it when I feel like I can, but that's not going to happen now.

I'm grateful to have friends like you, though. Right now, just knowing someone cares is more than enough. Thank you so much!" Tears run down Kaylee's cheeks. You hug her.

Nothing else is said, and you both ride home on the bus, seated next to each other in silence.

You don't let on about what you saw. She is hurt by something and wants to be left alone. You think you know a little bit more from following Kaylee on this bus trip, but you still don't know enough.

When you get off the bus, you offer to meet up with her after school on Monday.

She declines saying, "No, sorry I have other things to do right now."

What happens next is up to you! It's time to choose a path.
You Think You Know Kaylee's Secret. Begin story 14 part 2 on **page 130.**

To learn Kaylee's Secret, skip ahead and read story 15 on **page 131**, then you can see if your guess was correct by reading 14 part 2, on **page 130.**

She just can't tell. Everyone will think this was her fault. They might call her names or even worse, tell her parents. She knows that people will soon find out that she's pregnant. The baby will grow, and it will be obvious. She won't tell who the father is. No, she can't. He said he was going to run away with her. But now that Kaylee found his profile, with his wife and his kids, she knows he never will.

He will never claim Kaylee or the baby. She trusted him. But now, she is still in middle school, *with a baby coming!*

How can she tell her parents this horrible secret? How can she tell *him?* How can she continue with an unborn baby inside her?

She was wrong to trust Nick. She never once thought that it wasn't her fault. It was. She should have known better. He made her feel so safe. So well loved!

These days she doesn't feel well. She can hardly fit into any of her clothes. Can she switch to an online school? It would be much easier to face a computer and a teacher who only sees her from the chest up.

There is no escaping this. Kaylee needs to find someone she can trust with her secret. She decides to call her older sister. Her sister has two kids. She will know what to do.

Kaylee sends a text, "Sharon, I have a problem and I need to tell someone. I need your help. Can I come over so we can talk?"

This story continues on page 140.

Her sister tells her that she can come over at any time. Kaylee catches a bus and arrives at her sister's house, within the hour.

Sharon stops what she's doing and welcomes her sister. Kaylee turns red, and it seems that her heart might be beating double time.

Sharon is concerned. "Kaylee, what is it. You know you can talk to me."

"Sharon, I have a big problem. I, I think I'm pregnant. I know I'm pregnant."

"Honey? How, What, Who? Who is the father? If he's your age, that is a problem because a kid your age couldn't support a baby."

"No, he's not. He's older."

"Older? How much older are we talking about?"

"Well, he told me he was twenty, but I know he's older than that. I found his Facebook profile."

"How did you meet him? Online?"

"Yes, Sharon. I met him online. I've been seeing him and going out while mom was working. I thought I was in love. I also thought he was in love with me."

Sharon shakes her head in disbelief.

"Once when I met up with him, he gave me a fake ID with my name and a birthdate that lined up with me being twenty-one. After that, we went out to a bar where he ordered me drinks."

This story continues on page 141.

Kaylee continues, "…I got so drunk that I don't even remember what happened. He must have taken my phone and texted Mom to tell her I was staying overnight at my friend Mia's house. That way when I didn't come home; Mom didn't know I had been out all night with Nick."

Sharon stops her and gives her a big hug. "Kaylee, what a jerk. He is older and he is trying to ruin your life!"

Kaylee is feeling numb. She feels like she can't even make the tears come anymore. "I know. He must have done that more than once because I remember

waking up in a bed, next to him in the morning. He would make me breakfast and then drive me home."

"I wonder if he drugged you or if that was just alcohol," says Sharon. "Where were you staying when you woke up?"

"I was in a house," Kaylee replied. "If it was his house, no one else was there."

"Show me, your phone Kaylee. First show me his picture on your messages and show me what he told you about himself."

Kaylee scrolls through her messages:

Hey Baby, you're cute. Want to meet up?
Sure, my name is Kaylee. What's your name?
I'm Nick, Nick Carpenter. How old are you?
I'm fourteen.
That's great because I'm twenty.
Where do you want to meet?

This story continues on page 142.

How about the Mall food court at 4:00.

Sure, see you then.

Her sister reads through this and many more messages and then asks to see the profile Kaylee found on Facebook.

Sharon's mouth drops open when she sees that it's the same guy, only he has a family. Kaylee also shows her the wife's profile where she inherited a horse ranch.

"Kaylee, this guy has lied to you about who he is. Even if he were twenty, he would be too old for you. But now that you know he has a family, and his wife has money, I'm pretty sure he won't leave her to run away with you."

Kaylee hangs her head. "I know. I was so stupid. I am in big trouble, and I know he won't help me."

Staring angrily at Nick's picture, Sharon clenches her fist.

"He can't help you, Kaylee. What he committed was a criminal act. He lied to you. He's a child predator. You are lucky that you found the guy on Facebook, though. There are a few things that need to happen now: you need to report this. Report him and tell the police what he did to you. I'm sending all these messages to myself, so we have them as backup.

You *will* need to talk to mom, though." Sharon reaches down and touches Kaylee on her belly. "You are at least three or maybe four months pregnant. You are going to have this baby, whether you keep it or not."

This story continues on page 143.

"Sharon, I didn't want to tell mom. That's why I told you."

"I know," Sharon replied, ". . .but I'm not your mother, and you really need your mother now. Mom will know what to do. She will make sure you have good prenatal care, which involves taking vitamins, and going to doctor visits.

I, on the other hand, will help you go to the police and file a report against Nick. I'm not your legal guardian so you need Mom for any paperwork involved in pressing charges. We will give a detective all the information you have."

"I don't want to go to the police, Sharon, Kaylee stammered. "This is my fault, not his and I don't want the man I love to get in trouble."

"The man you *love* knew he was in love with a *little girl*." Sharon replied.

"You are innocent. You didn't lie about your age. He knew you were fourteen before he arranged to meet you. He broke the law. Now there will be a baby. He should have thought about that sooner.

The baby will have his DNA and there will be proof that he is the father of a child, with a child. Nothing, not even love, promises or commitment will change the fact that you are underage. You were a minor before he met you and you still are. What he did is a criminal act."

This story continues on page 146.

"What did he tell you?"

"He said he loved me, and we were going to run away together. That's why I was crying. He isn't *my* father, he's my *baby's* father. He has kids and a wife with a horse ranch so why would he choose me? Now, I'm a fourteen-year-old, with a baby coming. But he will pay for this! He will probably get prison time."

"It's a good thing his wife can support herself and her family, with the horse ranch," you say.

You are so glad that Kaylee is doing okay. At least she is getting help now. It must have been so lonely and scary to carry her secret alone.

Kaylee signs up for an online school. She has the baby and chooses to give her up for adoption. Kaylee and her mother are hoping that she can get past this life shattering experience, if she doesn't have to raise a baby on her own.

Nick is arrested and taken into custody. During the court case, Nick is also charged with enticing and luring a minor.

Other cases are brought forward, and he has had relationships with two other minors. Kaylee doesn't have to worry about ever running into Nick again.

The next year, Kaylee comes back to school and your friendship continues. The next time you and your friends talk about boys you have a crush on, Kaylee admits that there's a boy her age that she really likes.

The End 24

Kaylee has been carrying around a horrible secret. Her secret is one that she could not solve on her own. She finally decided to tell someone safe. Someone who would help her and not blame her for what has happened. Kaylee has confided in her older sister who has children of her own. Now Kaylee will get the help she needs, not only with her unborn child, but with the law. Nick is a child predator. Even though he is married and has a family, he went onto a dating site to find and entice a young girl, to get her drunk and to have sex. What Nick did is a criminal act, and it is important to involve the law so that this man is stopped from ruining the lives of any other innocent, young girls.

The End 24

You have just learned about Kaylee's secret in story 15.
It's finally time for Kaylee to meet up with you again and tell her secret in person.
To read the final chapter of Keeping Secrets,
Does Kaylee Tell You Her Secret? Begin story 16 on **page 124.**

They talk about what is going on and how Ava needs to get to know her mom and her younger siblings. The next time Ava goes to stay with her mom for the summer, her younger brother and sister are there for the first two weeks. They plan a vacation together and visit a beach town nearby.

Ava is doing much better now. Everyone in her family is talking to each other. Not only does Ava have a relationship with her parents and siblings, but she is also living with her grandparents, where she feels the most at home.

Whenever Ava feels sad or helpless, she can talk to her counselor, her parents or her grandparents. She is no longer alone and no longer feels suicidal.

The End 16 &17

You have just finished reading about Ava's secret in story #11. It's time to choose a new path and learn another secret.
To read, What Is Kaylee Hiding? Begin story 12 on **page 16.**
Or learn Harper's Guess about what Kaylee's secret might be. Begin story 13 on **page 23.**

Keeping Secrets Footnotes:

#1 Story 1 When you need help with homework: The ten best sites for homework   help
https://www.educatorstechnology.com/2018/05/10-excellent-websites-to-help-students.html

#2 Story 1 Layla's story: How divorce affects children

There is an increase in anxiety and depression in children when parents get divorced. Divorce often brings financial strain to the parents and social difficulty to their children. Children may believe that they are the cause of their parents' divorce. Feelings of guilt and shame can make them feel anxious,   and   depressed.
https://www.psychologytoday.com/us/blog/21st-century-childhood/202208/the-impact-divorce-children

#3 Story 2 Layla's story: Can a thirteen-year-old choose which parent to live with?

This is determined by the state—some states will consider the child's opinion at age 12 and in other states it's age 13 or 14. This decision is still determined by a judge. In the case of Layla's family, it was decided that Layla   and   her   brother   will   stay   with   their   father.
https://www.bryanfagan.com/blog/2022/january/can-a-13-year-old-choose-which-parent-to-live-wi/

 #4 Story 3 Everly's story: Everly decided to tell her secret to her pastor, who is a clergyman. This can be a minister, a pastor, a priest, a bishop, a rabbi,   or   an   imam.   Clergy   have   the   privilege   of   confidentiality.
https://www.agfinancial.org/resources/article/church-liability-clergy-privilege-confidentially-and-reporting

#5 Story 4 Everly's story: Juvenile penalties of grand theft auto. Depending on the unique nature of your juvenile grand theft auto case, a conviction could lead to one or more of the following legal penalties:
- Fines – Are common for juvenile theft crimes, but are usually smaller than adult fines.

- Restitution – Payment for damages caused by juvenile violations.
- Counseling – Psychiatric therapy, evaluation, or commitment.
- Probation – Temporary, court-ordered supervision outside of detention facilities.
- Detention – Part-time or full-time confinement in a youth center or juvenile home. The court will determine the length of time that seems appropriate.

https://www.adrasandaltiglaw.com/juvenile-joyriding-car-theft/

#6 Story 4 Everly's story: a counselor can give good advice, but there are times when they have to break their confidentiality agreement with a client and that is mandated by state law. https://www.simplepractice.com/blog/therapist-break-confidentiality/

#7 Story 4 Everly's story: How do you know if you are addicted?

- Loss of energy or motivation.
- Neglecting one's appearance.
- Spending excessive amounts of money on the substance.
- Obsessing about the next dose, ensuring a consistent supply of the substance.
- Worrying about the next source of the substance.

https://americanaddictioncenters.org/adult-addiction-treatment-programs/signs

#8 Story 5 Skylee's story: What is child abduction? **Child abduction** or **child theft** is the unauthorized removal of a minor (a child under the age of eighteen from the custody of the child's natural parents or legally appointed   guardians. https://en.wikipedia.org/wiki/Child_abduction.

#9 Story 6 Skylee's story: Why would a birth certificate be flagged?

The birth certificate of a missing person is flagged by the Missing

Children's Information Center. State and Local registrars shall *flag* the *birth certificate records* of the missing person so that whenever a copy of the birth certificate or information about the birth record is requested, the registrars shall be alerted to the fact that the certificate is that of a missing person. National Center *for Missing* and Exploited *Children* (NCMEC) ... National Crime *Information Center* (NCIC) database of the Federal Bureau of Investigation. https://namus.nij.ojp.gov/services/dna

#10 Story 6 Skylee's story: Skylee's parents kidnapped her when she was very young. If they are convicted of misdemeanor child abduction, the parents can be sentenced to up to a year in county jail, a $1,000 fine, or both. If convicted of a felony level child abduction, they will face two, three, or four years in a California state prison and a maximum fine of $10,000.
https://www.egattorneys.com/domestic-violence/child-abduction-california-penal-code-278

#11 Story 7 Mia's story: Mia found out that she doesn't have a legal obligation to "get involved" if she's a witness to a hit and run accident. It's up to her. Any information she can provide (description of the vehicle, description of the driver, how the accident happened) might be crucial in identifying the driver so that he can face the appropriate legal consequences of the hit and run accident.

- One other thing to note: If law enforcement, a victim, an insurance company, or an attorney know that you have witnessed the crime and determines that you may have information that can aid a criminal investigation, you may receive a subpoena. This is a legal order that requires you to appear in court or at some other proceeding. It's not a request, but an order. If you ignore the subpoena, you'll face a "contempt of court" charge or some other legal sanction. **legal consequences of a hit and run accident.** Legal Consequences of a Hit and Run Accident | AACA (all-about-car-accidents.com)

#12 Story 8 Mia's story: What penalties could Mia's brother face because of the hit and run accident? He could be charged with a misdemeanor or a felony.

- The penalties could range from losing a driver's license, losing insurance, and having fines from $5000-$20,000.
- Jail time could be from one year for a misdemeanor to up to fifteen years for a felony.
- Some lose their license for 6 months to a year and others for their lifetime.

The guilty party should hire a traffic accident attorney, or in some cases, they may need a criminal attorney.

https://www.nolo.com/legal-encyclopedia/consequences-hit-run-accident.html

#13 Story 9 Harper's Story: What is inappropriate touching? Inappropriate touching, or inappropriate contact, is often used to describe contact that is:

- Unwanted sexual intercourse or other sexual acts
- Unwanted touching of intimate areas of another's body, such as the breasts or buttocks
- Unwanted touching of non-intimate areas of another's body, depending on the circumstances
- Gestures or acts that could be interpreted as sexual solicitation
- Touching that is inappropriate based on relationship, for example, sexual touching involving an adult and a child

https://www.jpllaw.net/sex-crimes/inappropriate-touching

#14 Story 9 Harper's Story: Child sexual abuse is defined as sexual activity with a child by an adult, adolescent, or older child. If any adult engages in sexual activity with a child, that is sexual abuse. https://www.preventchildabusenc.org/resource-hub/about-child-sexual-abuse/

#15 Story 10 Your Mom Tells Her Secret: What your mom saw led to an arrest of a child sex ring. This is a story from the news about a child sex ring: In a child pornography case in Texas. 28 children were rescued, and 59 adults were arrested for possession of digital material. https://www.nbcdfw.com/news/local/two-dozen-children-rescued-59-arrested-in-massive-child-porn-investigation-police/3197749/

#16 Story 11 Ava's Story: If you or someone you know suffers from depression and suicidal thoughts: call 988 which is the Suicide and Crisis Lifeline. The hours are: Available 24 hours. Languages: English, Spanish. If you witness suicidal behavior or hear someone speak about suicide, never promise to keep this secret.

#17 Story 11 Ava's Story: If you or someone you know is having suicidal thoughts, contact the **National Suicide Prevention Lifeline** at **988** for support and assistance from a trained counselor. If you or a loved one are in immediate danger, call 911.
https://www.verywellmind.com/suicidal-thoughts-and-depression-in-children-1066661

#18 Story 12 What is Kaylee Hiding? The following is a bullying story from the news: There were three friends. One boy paid his friend $20 to beat up the other boy. After the beating, they put him in the bed of a truck and took pictures, which were sent out on the internet. The boy who was beaten had damage to his eyesight, his hearing and a broken neck. Now his family is suing for millions. Before this beating, the boy had a promising career as a baseball pitcher. Now he has lost that opportunity. https://www.insider.com/tennessee-teenager-kelsey-mooore-assault-bet-suing-millions?amp&utm_source=taboola

#19 Story 12 What is Kaylee Hiding? Dealing with Steroid use in girls: Steroid users are more likely to have participated in high-school sports, used other illicit substances, and engaged in other risky behaviors. Individuals are likely to begin steroid use in their late teenaged years and their twenties. https://www.acog.org/clinical/clinical-guidance/committee-opinion/articles/2011/04/performance-enhancing-anabolic-steroid-abuse-in-women

#20 Story 12 What is Kaylee Hiding? Steroid medications affect metabolism, the way the body stores fat, and the distribution of fat in the body. Taking steroid medications can therefore lead to an increased appetite, leading to weight gain. Taking steroids long-term can lead to deposits of fat in the abdominal area. https://www.buzzrx.com/blog/do-steroids-make-you-gain-weight

#21 Story 13 Harper's Guess about runaways: A runaway is a minor (someone under the age of 18) who leaves home without a *parent's or guardian's* permission and is gone from the home overnight. https://www.criminaldefenselawyer.com/crime-penalties/juvenile/running-away.htm
Minors run away for complex reasons. The National Center for Missing and Exploited Children and the National Runaway Safeline have identified factors that put youth at an increased risk of running away:

- family dynamics (divorce, remarriage, problems with siblings, foster care)
- abuse (physical, sexual, emotional, verbal) and neglect

- alcohol and drug use
- suicidal thoughts or behavior
- self-harm
- medical and mental health conditions, and
- conflict about sexual orientation or gender identity.

Endangered Runaways (missingkids.org)

#22 Story 13 Harpers Guess concerning tagging: Tagging on private property is called vandalism. Juvenile vandalism is often considered an intentional act of property damage, even if they didn't intend to damage the property. In the state of Florida, juvenile vandalism is one of the most common offenses committed by minors. Vandalism charges can impact a teen's ability to get accepted to a reputable college, get a job, and affect that teen's reputation for many years to come.

- In the state of Florida, the minor may be required to pay restitution to the property owner.
- The minor may be sentenced to juvenile probation for 12 or more months.
- If this is not your first offence, you may be sentenced to time in a juvenile detention center.

https://www.defendyourbrowardcase.com/blog/2020/october/the-consequences-of-juvenile-vandalism/

#23 Story 14 You Think You Know Kaylee's secret, concerning adoption and finding her birth parents. https://creatingafamily.org/adoption-category/adoption-blog/what-adoptees-want-adopted-parents-to-know-about-adoption-reunions/

#24 Story 15 Kaylee's Secret: About minors going on dating sites: An online predator may be luring a child—Even though dating sites have age restrictions that don't allow anyone under the age of 18 to use their site, many underage kids have accessed these sites. It is very dangerous for these underage teens because many of those using these sites have also lied about their age. A teen boy who is listed on the site, may really be an adult male who is looking to lure a teen girl for sexual reasons.

https://www.theatlantic.com/family/archive/2022/06/teens-minors-using-dating-apps-grindr/661187/

Helpful information for teens and their families:

Homework help: Here is a list of ten helpful sites for Homework help:

- Brainly
- Chegg
- Socratic
- Quizlet
- Bartleby
- Numerade
- Schmoop
- Enotes
- Sparknotes
- Khan Academey

https://www.educatorstechnology.com/2018/05/10-excellent-websites-to-help-students.html

If you or someone you know is talking about suicide: Call the National Suicide hotline:
call 988 for help

If you or someone you know has run away or is talking about running, call The **National Runaway Safeline (NRS)** serves as the communication system for runaway and homeless youth. NRS provides free, confidential advice and referrals to local services for runaways and their parents and guardians in all 50 US states.
Call 1-800-RUNAWAY for immediate assistance.

If you or someone you know might have a drug or alcohol problem: contact **AA, NA or alateen**, https://alcoholicsanonymous.com/find-a-meeting/
or call the treatment hotline at:
800-839-1686
Or talk to a counselor, a priest or someone you can trust to help you.

If you have been sexually assaulted: The National Sexual Assault Telephone hotline
800 656 Hope (4673) will keep your information confidential and direct your call to a local sexual assault service provider in your area.
Calling the National Sexual Assault Hotline gives you access to a range of free services including:

- Confidential support from a trained staff member
- Support finding a local health facility that is trained to care for survivors of sexual assault and offers services like sexual assault forensic exams
- Someone to help you talk through what happened
- Local resources that can assist with your next steps toward healing and recovery
- Referrals for long term support in your area
- Information about the laws in your community
- Basic information about medical concerns

If you are a witness to a crime, call your local police station and ask to speak to the tipline. You can remain anonymous. Or **call 911** for immediate help.

If you know about a case of child pornography, call The National Center for Missing and Exploited Children our hotline
1-800-THE-LOST or 1 800 843-5678 is available 24 hours, 7 days a week and our staff are here to connect you to the resources you need.

Bring an Author to Your School

Author Jill Ammon Vanderwood is on a Speaking Media Tour to schools around the country. She can do school assemblies, library, or classroom visits in person or over Zoom.

Please contact the author if you would like to bring her to your school to present her program: Off Target—based on her book about gun safety, where the author helps students to answer these questions: What would you do if someone showed you a loaded gun? Or, what would you do if you thought a friend planned to take a gun to school?

On the Rocks program is for boys, and Cheers is for girls. These programs can be combined. These programs help a student answer the questions: What would you do if someone offered you an alcoholic drink? What if you went to a party and someone passed out from too much alcohol? Would you call 911 to get help, or run away so you wouldn't get in trouble? Should you ever get into a car with a drunk driver?

Jill has a brand-new program called Keeping Secrets—based on this book. This program explores what to do if you promised to keep a secret, but you know that someone's life is in danger. Is a secret a secret no matter what? Is it worth risking a friendship if you can save a life? And where can you get confidential help?

For more information about Jill Ammon Vanderwood or her books, visit jillvanderwood.com

To contact Jill Vanderwood: email brightonsbooks@gmail.com

Please put in the subject line: Bring an Author to My School. Send your name, at least your first name, the name of your school, the city and state you are in, the name of your principal or the person to contact, and a contact phone number.

Jill Ammon Vanderwood

Jill Ammon Vanderwood is the author of fourteen books, including her latest series, The Path You Choose, which includes the topics of gun safety, and underage drinking.

Her first book was published when she was in her fifties and was inspired by her grandchildren. Since then, she has been writing and publishing a new book nearly every year. She loves interacting with students in schools, reading her books to students and presenting school assemblies.

Jill is active in her writing circles and busy with her quilt guild. Her husband and family are her main joy and motivation.

Awards Won by Author Jill Ammon Vanderwood

- Indie Excellence Award
- Indie Excellence Award Finalist
- Best Books Award
- Teen Development Award
- 3-time Gold Quill Award winner from the League of Utah Writers
- 1 Silver Quill Award from the League of Utah Writers
- The Writer of the Year Award from the League of Utah Writers

2 Silver Awards from the International Mom's Choice Awards

Kerah Diez

Kerah Diez has been working with illustrations and graphics since 2006.

She is of Peruvian descent and grew to appreciate traditional and modern art from different countries and cultures. Kerah's understanding of cultures and art has greatly influenced her art pieces today.

Over the years, she has illustrated several books for author Jill Ammon Vanderwood. Their joint efforts for the picture book, Santa's Mysterious Boot: Finding the True Spirit of Christmas, have won this team a Gold Quill Award from the League of Utah Writers.

Kerah is now working on illustrations for classic tales with a South American and Peruvian twist.

Kerah's work is available on Instagram @kyu10art

www.ingramcontent.com/pod-product-compliance
Lightning Source LLC
Chambersburg PA
CBHW052000220626
47052CB00004B/1026